He Was A Cowboy In The City.

Everything about the man looked hopelessly out of place amid the chic uproar of the lively bar scene. It wasn't just the stitched leather boots, the close-fitting jeans or the yoked, western-style shirt that set him apart from the designer suits that filled the bar. Even if Garth Saxon had been wearing a European-cut sport coat, Italian shoes and a Swiss watch, he would have stood out in the San Francisco crowd.

Saxon was wide open spaces, harness leather and the kind of strength that seemed to come from the land itself. Surrounded by a flock of bright, chattering apartment dwellers busily intent on impressing one another with their stylish success, he was, indeed, unique.

From her vantage point across the bar, Devon Ellwood took one look at him and knew her year of freedom was about to come to an end.

He was here tonight to claim his bride.

Dear Reader:

Welcome! You hold in your hand a Silhouette Desire—your ticket to a whole new world of reading pleasure.

A Silhouette Desire is a sensuous, contemporary romance about passions, problems and the ultimate power of love. It is about today's woman—intelligent, successful, giving—but it is also the story of a romance between two people who are strong enough to follow their own individual paths, yet strong enough to compromise as well.

These books are written by, for and about "every woman that you are"—wife, mother, sister, lover, daughter, careerwoman. A Silhouette Desire heroine must face the same challenges, achieve the same successes, in her story as you do in your own life.

The Silhouette reader is not afraid to enjoy herself. She knows when to take things seriously, and when to indulge herself in a fantasy world. With six books a month, Silhouette Desire strives to meet her many moods, but each book is always a compelling love story.

I'm sure you'll enjoy *Saxon's Lady* by bestselling author Stephanie James. It is a wonderful story about a rugged rancher who discovers that the woman of his dreams has a will—and a way—of her own.

I also hope that once you say goodbye to Saxon and his lady, you'll say hello to another Silhouette book, and find yourself going wild . . . with Desire!

Best,

Isabel Swift
Senior Editor & Editorial Coordinator

STEPHANIE JAMES
Saxon's Lady

Silhouette Desire

Published by Silhouette Books New York

America's Publisher of Contemporary Romance

SILHOUETTE BOOKS
300 East 42nd St., New York, N.Y. 10017

ISBN: 0-373-48213-2

First Silhouette Books Desire Sampler edition
printing August 1987

America's Publisher of Contemporary Romance

Printed in the U.S.A.

STEPHANIE JAMES

loves good pasta, good wine and good romance. She considers herself a professional daydreamer and feels fortunate to have found an occupation that allows her to use her skills in that field. She and her husband, Frank, share a waterfront condo with their bird, Ferd. Ms. James also writes as Jayne Castle and Jayne Ann Krentz.

One

Everything about the man looked hopelessly out of place amid the chic uproar of the lively after-work bar scene. It wasn't just the stitched leather boots, the close-fitting denim pants or the yoked, Western-Style shirt that set him apart from the designer suits that filled the bar. Even if Garth Saxon had been wearing a European-cut sport coat, Italian shoes and a Swiss luxury watch he would have stood out in the San Francisco crowd. He was a cowboy in the city.

Saxon was wide-open spaces, harness leather and the kind of strength that seemed to come from the land itself. Surrounded by a flock of bright, chattering apartment dwellers busily intent on impressing one another with their stylish success, he was, indeed, unique.

From her vantage point across the bar Devon Ellwood took one look at him and knew her year of freedom was about to come to an end.

"Devon?" Christy Atkins leaned forward to make herself heard above the din. "Is something wrong?"

Devon jerked her gaze back to her attractive blond friend, aware that Saxon hadn't yet spotted his quarry. "What? Oh, no, Christy. I just saw someone I know. I suppose I'd better go invite him to join us. Do you mind?"

"Not if he's less than fifty."

"He's thirty-six."

"Well within the ballpark." Christy grinned good-naturedly and turned around to spot the newcomer. Her lavishly made-up eyes widened when she caught sight of the man filling the doorway. "Oh, my goodness. Not our usual style, is he? Are your tastes becoming kinky in your old age, Devon?"

Devon winced and got to her feet. "That's not a nice thing to say to someone who's just turned twenty-seven. You know what a sensitive soul I am. Excuse me a minute. I'll be right back."

"Make sure he scrapes his boots at the door."

Devon was surprised to find her response to Christy's small joke was unexpectedly defensive. "Don't worry," she told her friend coolly, "any dirt on Garth Saxon will be honest, clean dirt, unlike a lot of the stuff that sticks to some of these people." She tilted her chin slightly to indicate the crowd around them.

"Hey, I'm sorry," Christy apologized quickly. "I didn't mean to offend."

Devon summoned a wry, reassuring smile. "I know. I shouldn't have snapped at you. Hold on to our table, I'll just be a moment." She dived into the crowd, weaving an erratic path toward the door. Garth hadn't moved. He was still surveying the jungle of up-and-coming executives and office workers who had gathered in the stylish pub to celebrate the end of another workday.

As she made her way toward him, Devon chided herself for the abruptness of her response to her friend. There'd been no need to defend Garth Saxon. The man could most certainly take care of himself and anyone else around him. Furthermore, he tended to do exactly that—even though those around him hadn't always requested help and even though they didn't always appreciate Saxon's idea of what was best for them. Garth exercised the authority that came naturally to him with a calm certainty that inevitably made others give way. Devon knew from experience it could be maddening.

She acknowledged that it was tension as much as anything that had made her snap at Christy. She'd been telling herself all week that Garth wouldn't really show up today. But a part of her had known all along she was lying to herself. Maybe that was why she'd come to the singles bar with Christy after work instead of going straight home to her apartment. She'd been subconsciously trying to hide.

She should have known she couldn't hide from Garth.

But the logical, rational part of her had been so sure the year of freedom would have done its job, so certain that the rash promise she'd made exactly 364 days ago would have been forgotten.

She knew now she shouldn't have tried to delude herself. There was an inexorable, granite-hard quality about Garth Saxon that very little in life could affect. Nothing less than a volcanic explosion could make him deviate from his chosen path—and even then, he'd probably just make a slight detour to get to his goal.

In this case the goal was Devon Ellwood. *What a fool I was* Devon thought in sudden realization. She'd almost convinced herself that after a year Saxon would reconsider. *I should have known better.* But a year ago twelve months of freedom had stretched out before her looking like a lifetime. Anything could happen in a year. Minds could be changed and promises induced by passion could be forgotten. A man like Garth could be made to realize that Devon Ellwood wasn't really the right woman for him.

But here he was—every lean, tough, smoothly muscled inch of him. At six feet there were a lot of inches to Garth Saxon, Devon reflected. There was also a lot of strength and masculine heat and the kind of gentleness that could steal away a woman's breath.

Devon recalled rough-tipped fingers moving with exquisite care along the inside of her thigh; the unbearably exciting feel of Garth's teeth on her shoulder; the heavy, demanding weight of him as he covered her body with his own and the soft, deep, reassuring voice as he slowly and deliberately took possession of her.

I'll give you your year, sweetheart. But when it's over, I'm going to bring you home.

Devon felt the warmth rising in her and hurriedly caught her vagrant thoughts. Instinctively she shied away from the disturbing memories that threatened to crowd into her head. For a year she'd been keeping those memories carefully contained behind a locked door in her mind. But Garth's appearance in the bar this evening had set them free.

Saxon was studying the other side of the room now. Devon used the time to examine his blunt, raw-edged profile. There was no question of masculine beauty here, except, perhaps, for the eyes. His face had probably been carved by the same unforgiving hand that had been used to whittle mountains in its spare time. There was an unyielding strength in the line of his jaw and his bold cheekbones. His thick, dark brown hair was cut in a short, thoroughly practical style. The only softness in his face was the dark fringe of lashes that shadowed his clear, gray eyes. Heat burned again in Devon's cheeks as she briefly remembered the sizzling intensity that could light Garth Saxon's eyes.

At that instant Garth turned and caught sight of her moving toward him. When she saw the depths of the calm determination in his gaze Devon finally realized just how much of a fool she'd been to think that a year would make any difference at all to Garth Saxon. He hadn't forgotten the promise he'd coaxed from her in that one night of seemingly endless passion.

"I'll give you the time you think you want. A year of freedom," he'd bargained, "and when it's over we'll be married."

And Devon, burning brilliantly in the flames of a need she'd never before experienced, had agreed. Regret hadn't set in until the next day. By then it was too late. Garth Saxon's word was bankable. He expected others to keep their promises, too.

He was here tonight to claim his bride.

Devon controlled her instinct to flee, knowing that such a reaction would be totally useless. Saxon would simply come after her. He would use the same gentle, calm, inexorable determination to chase after a recalcitrant woman as he used to train his magnificent Arabian horses. The end result would be the same. Ultimately, the woman would surrender to the inevitable, just as the horse always did.

Her only hope, Devon told herself wildly, lay in being cool and rational and unemotional. She must make Garth understand what she'd been certain of a year ago. There might be passion between them but they weren't right for each other—she wasn't the kind of wife he needed and he wasn't the kind of man she might someday want to marry. If she ever married at all.

Devon emerged from the protective cover of the crowd and summoned a bright, charming smile as she came to a halt in front of Garth.

"You forgot your hat," she said lightly, thinking of the rather battered Stetson he was seldom without. As an opening remark, it probably lacked wit, but Devon couldn't think of anything else to say. The tension in her was making it difficult to think clearly.

"It's out in the truck." Garth was the kind of man who took most things, including questions, literally. "I got the feeling it wouldn't look quite right in here."

He was devouring the sight of her, taking in first the sassy, blow-dried style of her shoulder-length hair, tawny-brown hair. When she had left Hawk Springs a year ago, her long hair had been parted in the middle and worn in a neat coil at the back of her neck.

Her hairstyle wasn't the only thing that had changed about her during the past year, Devon knew. The brilliance of her coral-red lipstick and the artfully applied mascara and blusher that highlighted the antique-gold of her eyes were also new additions. She was five feet, five inches tall, but the heels of her stylish leather pumps gave her another couple of inches. She could have used a few more in dealing with Garth, she decided.

In Hawk Springs Devon had worn either jeans or a practical skirt and blouse most of the time. She wasn't wearing jeans tonight. She had come directly from the office after work and still wore the sleek, narrow black skirt, long-lined black and white jacket and topaz-yellow silk blouse she'd worn all day. She had bought the outrageously expensive suit just last week, pleased with the way it glided over her slender figure. The padded shoulders gave her a little extra width on top that she thought she needed to disguise the decidedly dainty contour of her breasts. Somehow the long, floating jacket seemed to emphasize her small waist and neatly rounded hips.

If Garth ever learned the price of the outfit he would be stunned. Garth Saxon was a financially successful man but he had a rancher's staid, old-fashioned ideas about money. Money was to be invested in land and horses and equipment, not frivolous designer clothing.

"I'm having a drink with a friend," Devon said finally in an attempt to interrupt Garth's endless perusal of her new image. "Why don't you join us?"

"A friend?"

She saw the flicker of disapproval in his gaze and unthinkingly rushed to explain. "A female friend. A coworker. Come on, Garth, you look like you could use a drink." Impulsively Devon reached out to catch hold of his hand and lead him back through the crowd. Her spirits lifted as the initial shock began to wear off.

This was her world, her environment. Here, she was in control and at home. Garth had too much quiet self-confidence to ever feel truly awkward in a social situation, but there was no doubt that he must be feeling at least slightly out of step with those around him. Devon decided to capitalize on that small fact. As she started to guide him through the crush, however, she felt a slight resistance on the other end of the hand she was holding. A slight resistance from Garth meant everything slowed to a full stop. Devon glanced back at him inquiringly.

"I think we ought to leave, Devon. We have a lot to talk about and I'd rather have a drink at your place where I can relax. I've had a long drive and I'm not feeling too social."

"My drink just arrived, Garth. I haven't had more than a sip. You wouldn't want me to waste my money, would you? Besides, I can't just walk out on Christy. It wouldn't be polite. I have to at least say goodbye." She tugged again and this time he reluctantly followed. His big hand enveloped hers and she could feel the calluses on his palm. Garth had always worked hard for the good living he made.

"One drink, Devon. That's all we have time for this evening."

She stifled a sigh and tried for a teasing smile, instead. "Same old Garth. Always giving orders."

"I wasn't giving orders," he protested as the crowd parted easily to let him through, "I was just pointing out that we don't have a lot of time. I want to get back to the ranch tomorrow. Are you all packed?"

"Uh, not exactly, Garth . . ."

His reaction was immediate and forceful. "What the hell do you mean, not exactly? You've had all the time in the world to get ready. I sent you a note last week reminding you I'd be here today."

Devon remembered the note. Her breath had caught in her throat when she'd opened her mailbox to find a plain white envelope addressed in Garth's bold scrawl. The message inside had been brief and to the point. He had told her he would be arriving Monday evening. Implicit in the short message was the understanding that she would be ready to leave San Francisco.

Even with the note in her hand, Devon hadn't quite believed he would just show up as if everything between them really was well and firmly settled. Surely a year had made some difference. Surely it had caused him to reflect on the plans he'd made and the promise he'd persuaded her to give. Surely he'd found someone else in a year's time.

Christy's eyes were bright with humor and curiosity as Devon and Garth approached the table. She scanned Garth appraisingly as Devon made introductions.

"Christy, this is Garth Saxon. He's a, uh, friend of mine from Hawk Springs. He owns an Arabian stud farm there called Hawk's Flight. Christy Atkins, Garth. She works out of the same temporary-help agency that I do, Garth. We've both been assigned to the same accounting firm this past week. When we finished for the day, we decided to drop in here for a drink."

Garth nodded with a kind of old-fashioned formality that was second nature to him. "Miss Atkins."

"Call me Christy and please sit down. I managed to commandeer an extra chair. How did you find Devon tonight? Did you know she would be here?"

"I got into the city a little early. I phoned the temp agency and they told me where she was working. I decided to drive straight to the office and try to catch her before she left for the day. I was too late, obviously, but someone there thought she might have come over here after work." Garth paused as the cocktail hostess halted by the table. "I'll have a beer."

The hostess nodded. "What kind, sir?"

Garth blinked slowly. "What kind have you got?"

"Ten domestic and twelve foreign. Would you like to see the list?" the hostess asked politely.

"A list? Just to order a beer? No thanks. Give me whatever's on draft."

"We have five labels on draft," the hostess assured him helpfully. She began to recite the names.

Garth cut her off with a small, chopping movement of his hand. He ordered the first one she'd named, looking relieved when the woman finally went away. His mouth curved ruefully as he glanced at the glass of white wine sitting in front of Devon. "If it's this hard to get a pint of beer here, I'd hate to try for a glass of wine."

"It takes a little practice, but you learn how to order what you want," Devon said softly. She picked up her glass and added just before she took a sip, "I've learned a lot of things like that this past year." She watched him from under her lashes as he absorbed the implications of the remark. She knew he understood what she was saying, but it didn't seem to faze him unduly. Garth wouldn't particularly care what upwardly mobile social graces she'd learned in the past twelve months. He didn't have much use for such niceties.

"I imagine you have." Garth shrugged as his beer arrived. "A year is a long time."

"What is all this about a year?" Christy demanded, glancing from Devon to Garth and back again.

"I've been away from Hawk Springs for a year," Devon rushed to explain. She didn't succeed in stopping Garth from adding his two cents' worth.

"Devon wanted a year of city life before she got married," he said casually to Christy.

"Before she got *married*?" Christy looked suddenly torn between shock and amusement, as if she were expecting Devon to tell her it was all a joke. "You never told me you had any marriage plans, Devon."

"It's a long story," Devon tried to say with a dismissive air.

Garth's eyes roved appraisingly over Devon's flushed face. "A year-long story," he agreed. "But it's finally finished."

"Devon, for crying out loud, tell me what's going on?" Christy looked fascinated. "Are you really going to marry this man?"

"Uh, it's not settled yet," Devon began, only to be interrupted by Garth.

"Of course, it's settled. That's why I'm here." He glanced at the stainless steel watch on his wrist. "When you finish playing with that glass of wine, Devon, we'll be on our way. Got a lot to do, from the sound of it." He shook his head in mild disgust. "I can't believe you haven't even started packing. We've got some work ahead of us this evening if we're going to be on the road tomorrow."

"On the road? But, Devon, what about your job?" Christy said a little helplessly.

Devon sighed. "I'm a temporary employee, remember? Here today, gone tomorrow. The agency won't have any trouble finding another substitute."

Devon knew she could have gotten a better job than the one she had. At several points during the past year employers who had used her temporarily had offered her full-time, permanent positions that would have offered good possibilities of advancement. Devon had told herself that one of these days she would take one of the offers. But she hadn't quite dared to until the year was over and she could be certain her freedom was for real. Devon sighed again, took another swallow of wine and watched her future waver in front of her like a fun-house mirror.

"Will one of you please tell me what this is all about?" Christy pleaded. "Devon, why are you marrying this man? You've never even mentioned him to me."

It was Garth who answered. "It's simple enough. She's marrying me because a year ago she promised she would. We've had an understanding between us."

Talk about having your fate sealed, Devon thought. "It's a little more complicated than that, Christy."

"But a year apart?" Christy eyed her friend consideringly. "It doesn't make any sense. If you two were engaged a year ago why on earth have you waited so long to get married?"

Garth hoisted his beer. "I agree with you, Miss Atkins. It doesn't make much sense. But that's the way Devon wanted it. In a way I guess I understood, but it's been a damn long year."

Christy pinned Devon beneath a demanding stare. "Tell me why you've been here in San Francisco for a solid year while your... your fiancé has been in Hawk Springs."

"Oh, Christy, it's really a long story and I don't think I can explain the whole thing right now."

Garth looked vaguely amused. "It's not all that complicated. I can explain it in twenty-five words or less."

"So explain!" Christy said.

Garth shrugged. "A year ago Devon was feeling trapped. She thought she'd been missing out on something and she wanted a year to find out what, exactly, she might have missed. I tried to tell her there wasn't anything out there she really needed, but she was like a high-strung filly with a burr under her saddle. Wouldn't listen to reason. So I let her go for a while."

"That's a lot more than twenty-five words," Devon mumbled. "A high-strung filly with a burr under my saddle? Garth, for heaven's sake..."

Christy's gaze swung to Devon. She ignored her friend's muttered comment and went right to the point. "Why were you feeling trapped?"

Helplessly Devon slid a sidelong glance at Garth who appeared totally unperturbed by the relentless questioning. As far as he was concerned everything was settled now. In a few minutes he would be taking Devon back to her apartment. Then he would organize the packing in his usual efficient, methodical style, and when it was done he would load Devon and her baggage into the truck and take both back to Hawk Springs. Devon could read the inexorable flow of his thoughts as clearly as if he'd spoken them aloud.

Perhaps it was the mounting sensation of being locked into a preordained pattern of events that made Devon decide to answer Christy's questions. Anything to keep the conversation going and forestall the ultimate conclusion to this little scene.

"I was raised in Hawk Springs," Devon explained quietly. "It's a small farming and ranching community out in the Central Valley. A *very* small community."

"Truth is," Garth interjected easily, "it's a good size for a town. Everyone knows his neighbors. People look out for each other."

Devon raised her eyebrows in silent comment to Christy. "I'm sure you get the picture."

"Hicksville, U.S.A." Christy grinned.

"In a word, yes," Devon agreed, ignoring Garth's frown. "My parents had a small farm there. Personally, I couldn't wait to get away from the wonders of bucolic bliss. The instant I graduated from high school, I left for Los Angeles. I enrolled at the University of California and set to work on a nice, vague liberal arts degree with a fine arts minor."

Christy switched her attention to Garth for a few seconds. "Did you know her then?"

He shook his head. "No. I didn't move to Hawk Springs until two and a half years ago when I bought the stud farm. Unlike Devon, I already knew what the big city had to offer and I wasn't impressed."

Christy turned back to Devon. "All right, go on."

"During my junior year my parents were killed in an automobile accident." Devon heard her voice tighten and wondered at the reaction. Surely after all this time she had recovered from the shock and the trauma of the tragedy.

She broke off, collecting her thoughts, and in the brief silence Garth calmly reached out to cover her hand with his own.

"Devon has two brothers, Lee and Kurt," he explained to Christy. "They were both in their teens when their parents were killed. Devon left college to come back to Hawk Springs to take care of them. It wasn't an easy job. The boys were a handful and there were..." Garth hesitated, then said carefully, "money problems. She had to sell the farm to pay off some debts her dad had run up. She moved into town and took a job in the bank. But two years ago she got Kurt into college, and last year Lee started his freshman year. They're both on their own now, paying their way with jobs and a little cash Devon's folks had left in trust funds."

Understanding lit Christy's expression. She smiled at Devon. "So a year ago, you were finally free again."

Devon nodded, thinking of what that freedom had meant. At long last she had been free from the burden of scrimping and scraping to make ends meet on the pay she'd received from her clerical job at the bank. Free from having to lie awake at nights worrying about Lee getting into trouble with the law. Free from having to fret about Kurt's too-serious attitude toward life. Free from knowing everyone in town was waiting to see if she would get herself into trouble with a man.

She glanced at the hard profile of the man sitting beside her. That last worry had been a minor one until Garth Saxon had come along. She half smiled to herself. Even after he'd arrived in her life, Devon knew she hadn't had to worry overmuch about getting herself into trouble with a man. Garth was the soul of propriety. The last thing he would have done was expose her to gossip.

His attitude had been protective and supportive. He'd offered friendship when she had needed it most. That had been the year Lee had started running dangerously wild and Devon had faced the fact that she couldn't control her younger brother. Garth had stepped in and supplied the firm hand on the reins that the youth had needed. Lee had responded sullenly at first but the resentment had quickly turned to worship. The boy had turned into a man under Garth's guidance. For that reason alone, Devon knew she would always feel a deep sense of gratitude toward Garth Saxon. She owed him.

But it wasn't until the night she announced her intentions to shake the dust of Hawk Springs once more from her feet that Devon had finally understood what lay beneath Garth's protective friendship. He wanted her, and with his usual unfaltering decisiveness, he'd decided she would make him a good wife. He'd merely been biding his time.

Garth, too, had been waiting for Devon to be free, knowing she wouldn't consider marriage until her brothers had left home. It had been a shock for him, Devon realized, when he'd discovered she intended to use her freedom to flee to the glittering lights of San Francisco.

Garth had been shaken by her announcement. Devon suspected it was a measure of his shock that he'd actually set about deliberately seducing her that night. All the months of being so careful with her reputation, of walking the narrow line of friendship had gone up in flames when Garth had taken her in his arms and let the full force of his desire envelop her.

And Devon, to her lasting incomprehension and chagrin, had melted in his arms like warm honey. He wasn't right for her, nor she for him—or so she'd tried to tell herself. She was meant for city life and Garth was a man of the land. She'd tried telling him that, too, but he hadn't listened. He'd simply held her more tightly, touched her more intimately and, finally, taken her completely. Lost in the mind-spinning excitement of Garth's sensual possession, Devon had almost believed him when he told her they belonged together.

In the end the bargain had been struck. It had been all Devon could do to cling to a year of freedom. During those hours of raging passion she'd almost surrendered entirely. If she'd done so, she knew she would have been married a year ago. Garth Saxon was not a man to put off until tomorrow what he thought ought to be done today.

Days, weeks, months later she told herself it had all been a ghastly mistake, one Garth, himself, was certain to acknowledge as time passed.

But here he was, one year later to the day, expecting her to keep her rash promise. Even as the thought crossed her mind, she watched Garth glance again at his watch.

"It's time to go, Devon." He put down his empty glass and got to his feet. "Where's your coat?"

Devon's fingers shook slightly as she set her own glass down on the table with care. "On that hook over there." She indicated a brass hook on the wall that was buried under a variety of stylish trench coats and umbrellas. "The khaki one."

Garth followed her glance. "They're all khaki."

"It's the style, Garth. Sort of like cowboy boots back in Hawk Springs. Everyone wears them. My coat has a yellow scarf around the collar."

Christy watched him move purposefully across the room. Garth cut through the crowd with the ease of an Arabian stallion moving through a herd of Shetland ponies. Christy whistled soundlessly. "I can't believe this, Devon."

Devon collected her expensive leather clutch bag and rose to her feet. "Neither can I."

"Are you really going with him?"

Devon hesitated. "For now," she said softly. "I have to go with him Christy. Garth and I need to talk."

"I don't think talking is going to change his mind. That man's already waited a solid year. He wants you, Devon."

Devon tightened her grip on the leather clutch as she turned her head to watch Garth stride back toward them, khaki trench coat in hand. "We're all wrong for each other. But he doesn't seem to understand that. I'm city and he's country. Why can't he see that?"

"Probably," Christy remarked dryly, "because he's looking at something a bit more fundamental. He's a man and you're the woman he wants. I have a hunch that for him it's all fairly simple and straightforward. Do you love him, Devon?"

Devon was startled by the question. For an instant words deserted her. Then she said in a rush, "Love him? Christy, you don't seem to comprehend the situation. I've tried to explain..."

"I've known you for almost a whole year, Devon, and I would stake my next paycheck that you haven't let any man do more than give you a polite good-night kiss after a date. Your social life is active enough, but hardly passionate. You've got lots of friends, but no lovers. There's been more than one or two men this past year who would have been quite happy to receive an invitation to bed and even a serious relationship."

Devon was shocked. "I couldn't possibly have gotten involved in a serious relationship with any of the men I've been dating."

"Why not? Some of them were quite nice."

"Yes, but . . ." Devon's voice trailed off weakly as she realized just what she was tacitly admitting. There had been no other man for her this past year. She had told herself it was because she was too busy enjoying her freedom to get involved with a serious commitment. But deep down she knew there'd always been another reason for keeping her dates casual and uncomplicated.

There was no sense fooling herself. Subconsciously she'd been waiting for Garth.

"Well?" Christy prompted.

"It's crazy," Devon whispered in soft panic. She didn't want to think about Christy's question. "The whole thing is total nonsense. Don't you see, Christy? Garth and I are all wrong for each other."

She jumped as she felt Garth's hand on her shoulder. He settled the trench coat around her shoulders without a word. Mutely she glanced up at him, wondering how much he'd overheard. But he merely smiled slightly and nodded politely toward Christy.

Then he guided Devon gently but firmly toward the door as if she were a nervous little stray filly he'd rounded up to take home.

Two

Devon was still skittish, still looking for a way to avoid him, still clinging to her muddled notion of freedom, Garth thought as he guided the late-model pickup out of the downtown financial district. Perhaps a year's grace had been a mistake, after all.

It had certainly given her a sophisticated veneer, he had to admit. At a stoplight he examined her covertly as she sat beside him in the cab. She hadn't said a word since they'd left the pub. Mentally he cataloged the things about her that had changed. None of them mattered. Underneath she was still the gallant, vibrant woman who'd captivated him from the first moment they'd met. He sensed she would always have the power to make his body tighten with desire even as she aroused his protective instincts.

Objectively speaking, he knew she wasn't beautiful. There was an open, honest attractiveness about her that lacked the aloof mystery of classic beauty. He remem-

bered her in faded jeans that fit lovingly over her sweetly
curving hips. And he remembered the shape of those soft
thighs under his hands. She had felt so good, so soft and
sexy and she'd given herself so completely that night.

For a year Garth had been living with the white-hot
memories of the night he'd lost his self-control and taken
Devon to bed. The brilliance of her golden eyes as she'd
looked up at him from beneath her lashes had tormented
him for twelve long months. The vivid recollection of the
tight, throbbing feel of her clinging body had caused him
to spend more than one night since then lying awake in an
agony of frustration. At four in the morning he would
sometimes imagine he could hear the soft cries she'd made
when she'd shivered and convulsed in his arms. In the cold
hours before dawn he frequently found himself conjuring
up the memory of how it had felt to twist his hands deep
into her long tawny hair. That kind of imagination had
nearly driven him out of his mind at times.

Turning Hawk's Flight into a first-class stud farm had
been a sixteen-hour-a-day job since he'd bought the place
two and a half years ago. He probably could have relaxed
a little this past year as his plans for the ranch began to
take concrete shape. But he'd kept up the hard pace because he'd needed to work off the frustration of waiting
for Devon. Now, at last, the waiting was over.

"I liked your hair the old way," he stated suddenly as
the light changed.

Devon glanced at him and then back at the traffic in
front of the truck. "Do you? I like it this way. More modern."

"Probably more expensive, too," he remarked idly.

Her mouth curved in a secret little smile. "You're right.
I have to have it trimmed every six weeks and my stylist
costs a fortune."

"I doubt if Willy Mae is going to be able to keep it looking that way for you," Garth persisted. Willy Mae had been Hawk Springs's only hairdresser for the past fifteen years.

"You could be right," Devon said noncommittally. "Willy Mae peaked professionally just before she came to Hawk Springs. She hasn't done anything since to keep up with the latest styles. Everyone who comes out of her shop is at least fifteen years out of date. Take a left here."

"I remember," Garth said gently. He had only visited Devon once in her San Francisco apartment. That had been at Christmas when Lee and Kurt had told him they were going to be spending the holiday with their sister in the city. It hadn't taken much to get himself invited along. Devon had put up a tree, cooked a traditional meal and wrapped presents for everyone. It had been a cheerful, festive occasion. Afterward the three men had spent the night in sleeping bags in her small living room. The next day all three had left. Garth hadn't been able to think of an excuse to stay, and Devon hadn't asked him to remain behind after her brothers left. There had still been four months to go in her year of freedom and Garth had been bound by his end of the bargain.

Now, fifteen minutes after leaving the heart of the city, Garth finally found a space for the pickup in front of Devon's Victorian-style flat. It was typical of the apartments that lined the neighborhood streets. He opened the door of the truck and went around to Devon's side of the vehicle. She already had her door open by the time he got there. Devon had grown up in farming country where women didn't expect men to open pickup truck doors for them. Garth wondered if she'd been dating anyone who did open car doors. With her new tastes, they would have been Porsche doors.

"What's the matter, Garth?" Devon asked as she fished her keys out of the leather clutch and led the way toward the door. "You look as if you just found out one of your prize mares had decided to refuse a stallion you'd hand-picked for her."

His mouth twisted wryly. "I couldn't have looked that upset. I was just wondering about your social life this past year."

"It's been a fun year," Devon said firmly as she opened the front door and started up the stairs to her flat.

Garth felt something clench in his guts. "How much fun have you had, Devon?" he asked quietly as he followed her up the stairs.

Devon heard the coolness in the question and shivered a little as she opened her front door. "You don't have the right to ask any questions, Garth," she said softly. She stepped into her stylish, black-and-white living room, feeling more sure of herself in her own home. The apartment had been furnished to her taste with a white carpet, polished black furniture and here and there a dash of exotic, brilliant red.

Garth stood in the doorway, taking in the sophisticated room. "This place looked better at Christmas when you had a tree in the corner and some decorations around."

Devon shrugged, secretly relieved he was apparently not going to pursue his earlier question about her social life. "I like the sleek, modern look."

"I'll admit it's about as far away from Hawk Springs as you can get," he said with a glance that dismissed the entire apartment. His clear gray eyes caught and trapped her. "Just tell me the truth, Devon. It's been eating me alive."

She swallowed at the blunt honesty of the question. So much for hoping he wouldn't persist in his quest to find out about her social life. Garth never gave up until he had

the answers to his questions. To give herself time to think
of a light response, she walked toward the hall that led to
the single bedroom. Perhaps she should lie, tell him she'd
had other lovers this past year. It might solve the intoler-
able problem she faced. Then again, it might not. Garth
was a very persistent man. "Help yourself to a drink while
I change my clothes. I don't have any beer, but I've got
some wine. I'll start dinner as soon as I'm out of this suit."

"Devon."

He hadn't raised his voice behind her, but then, he didn't
need to. Garth Saxon had been in command of himself and
his world for so long that the habit of being in charge came
naturally to him. The habit of responding obediently came
just as naturally to those around him, Devon thought ruefully. She stopped and turned to face him. When she saw
the intent need to know in his eyes, her will to resist col-
lapsed. This was Garth. Whatever else came between them,
she wouldn't lie to him.

"I've gone out on a few dates," she said carefully, "but
I haven't... Oh, for heaven's sake, Garth. You know there
hasn't been anyone else. How could there be as long as we
had an understanding?"

He nodded, looking at once satisfied and complacent.
The intensity disappeared from his eyes. "I know, Devon. Guess I just wanted to hear you say it. There've been
times this past year when I thought I'd drive myself over
the edge wondering. Forget it. It's all over now, thank
God. I'll open some wine while you change. I'm looking
forward to some of your cooking."

Devon watched helplessly as he disappeared into the
kitchen. At Christmas when he'd been here he'd acted like
a guest. This evening he was acting as though he owned the
place. When she heard the sound of the refrigerator door

being opened, she whirled around and hurried down the hall to the safety of her bedroom.

Her odd state of ambivalence was annoying and disconcerting, she thought as she peeled off the black and white suit and hung the yellow silk blouse on a padded hanger. A part of her had known instinctively that Garth would show up today, but another part of her had been so certain that everything had changed during the past year and that somehow he would realize it.

Her present mood was precarious. She felt unnerved and uncertain. Garth was walking back into her life with his usual forthright, uncompromising manner, and even though she'd had a year to plan for this moment, she still wasn't sure how to handle it.

When she'd finished changing her clothes she wandered slowly back down the hall and into the kitchen. Standing in the doorway she watched Garth pour Johannesburg Riesling into two glasses. He always seemed to move in that slow, easy, deliberate way. It could be deceptive, Devon knew. When the occasion called for it, Garth could move with a blinding swiftness that was backed by a rawhide-tough strength.

He glanced up as she entered the kitchen. His gaze moved over the emerald silk blouse and then fell to the cream-colored designer jeans that hugged her derriere and tightly sheathed her legs all the way to her narrow ankles. Garth stopped when he reached the tiny, black ballet-style slippers she wore on her feet, and his eyes came back up to her face. There was a trace of amusement in his faint smile.

"Those fancy clothes would last about fifteen minutes back in Hawk Springs."

"I know." Devon took the glass he offered. "The reverse was true when I moved to San Francisco. I was embarrassed to be seen on the streets in my Hawk Springs clothes. This is a very sophisticated city."

Garth's eyes narrowed consideringly. "And you've learned to fit right in, haven't you, Devon?"

"I try," she said lightly. She was about to take a sip from the glass, but Garth stopped her by touching the rim of his glass to hers in a small, meaningful salute.

"To us, Devon," he said quietly. "It's been a long time."

She stared up at him, very aware of just how large he was. When he was gone, she could forget about his size and the carefully controlled power that radiated from him. But in person there was no way on earth to ignore it. "Yes," she said tonelessly, "it's been a long time."

They sipped their wine in silence for a moment until Devon grew too uneasy beneath the pressure of Garth's wordless intent. She could feel it reaching out to her, reestablishing connections she thought she'd broken this past year. Without even touching her he was making her vividly aware of the claim he had on her. Restlessly she moved to the refrigerator.

"Hungry?" Devon asked for want of anything more brilliant to say.

"Starving."

She sensed the double meaning behind the word and chose to ignore it. Instead she busied herself taking fresh ginger, daikon, sesame seed paste and peanut butter from the refrigerator. "So. Give me all the news. How are things back in Hawk Springs?"

"Pretty much the same as when you left."

Devon made a wry face as she closed the refrigerator and went to the cupboard for a package of thin noodles. "I could have guessed as much. Nothing ever changes back there. How's your brother?"

"Ryan?" Garth grimaced as he named his half brother. Ryan was a few years younger than Garth, close to Devon's age. "Nothing much changes with him, either. Still trying to make a fortune with computers. He still worries me at times."

"He's basically a good boy, Garth."

"That's his whole problem. He's still a boy. At his age, he ought to be settling down and acting like a man. He ought to be assuming responsibilities. He was raised on a cattle ranch, same as I was. He knows how to work for a living. He should have stuck to ranching instead of trying to make his way in something like computers. I probably should never have sent him to college."

"You're too hard on him." This was something she and Garth had in common, Devon acknowledged. Both of them, through slightly different sets of circumstances, had wound up being responsible for younger brothers.

In Garth's case it was because his widowed father had remarried a much younger woman and had another son. When Ryan was ten years old his mother had left, leaving Ryan to be raised by his father. Chase Saxon had done his best but something had gone out of him when his beautiful young wife had left him. He'd turned to the bottle with steady persistence and Garth had had to assume responsibility for the ranch and his younger half brother. Eventually the alcohol had killed the elder Saxon in the form of a collision with a tree on a lonely road at two in the morning.

"I might be hard on him if he were actually living at the ranch, but he's not. He's got a job in L.A. now," Garth said. "He tells me he's an account executive, whatever that is. I think it translates as computer salesman."

Devon was surprised. "Good for him," she said approvingly.

"We'll see. I'd be happier if he'd shaped up the way Lee did."

"My brother is a different kind of person. He needed guidance from a man, and when he got it he responded to it. What works with one type of human being doesn't necessarily work with another. Also, you're related to Ryan. That makes a difference, too. I think Ryan's always subconsciously trying to compete with you, trying to prove himself."

"Maybe." Garth looked skeptical. He wasn't big on psychological analysis. He preferred cold hard facts and concrete realities. He was good at dealing with that kind of thing.

"If he makes it on his own in L.A. he might be better equipped to handle his relationship with you—he needs to feel he can hold his own. In case you aren't aware of it, Garth, that's not an easy task."

He gave her his slow, rare grin. "Am I that intimidating?"

"You can be," she assured him.

"Well, you shouldn't have to worry about proving anything to me, Devon. You've already proved everything you'll ever need to prove to anyone, including yourself. There aren't a lot of young women who would have had the guts and the stamina to take on the responsibilities you took on after your folks were killed. Just look at what you accomplished. You paid off all your father's farm debts and kept yourself and your brothers afloat financially for five years, until you got both boys into college. Everyone in Hawk Springs knows it wasn't easy. And everyone in town knows you didn't go on welfare or take any charity to get by, either. You should be proud of what you did for yourself and Lee and Kurt."

"Mostly I'm just glad it's over," Devon told him with an unconscious sigh. "There were times when I thought I'd be trapped forever in Hawk Springs."

"You'll be able to appreciate it more now when you return," Garth said easily.

Devon slid him a quick, sidelong glance. "You didn't think I'd stay away the full year, did you, Garth?"

He shrugged. "I suppose I thought you'd get tired of big city life and come home before the year was out. You're a small-town girl at heart." He seemed totally oblivious to the sophisticated statement made by the apartment and her clothing.

"As it turned out," Devon said pointedly, "I discovered I love city life."

"I don't think so," Garth said judiciously, as if he'd given the subject a great deal of thought. "You just needed a change for a while. Or at least you thought you did. You wanted a break from all those years of struggling and worrying about Lee and Kurt. Hawk Springs will look different to you when you come back as my wife. You'll be able to think about your own life instead of spending all your time worrying about your brothers. That difference will change your opinion of the place. You'll see."

One of the most difficult things to fight in Garth was his habit of being utterly certain of his own decisions. Devon knew he never made them in haste. He always took his time, weighing every side of a question, analyzing all the aspects of it and finally arriving at the conclusion and a plan of action that was unshakable. The fact that he was almost always right in his decisions made him even more difficult to battle. Trying to deflect Garth from his chosen path was like standing in front of a herd of charging buffalo and yelling "Shoo." One could get trampled. Sane people got out of the way.

"Actually," Devon said as she dumped the noodles into boiling water, "I've been doing a lot of thinking about my life while I've been here in San Francisco."

"Yeah?" Garth sounded only politely interested.

"Yeah." She swung around to face him, bracing herself with her hands on the counter behind her. "Has it occurred to you, Garth, that we, that is you and me, might not, uh, be suited to each other?"

He took a long swallow of wine. "No." He reached for the bottle and refilled his glass.

In the face of that flat denial, Devon wasn't quite sure how to proceed. She cleared her throat. "Garth, be reasonable. We have a lot to think about, a lot to consider before we rush into marriage."

"I've spent the past twelve months considering the subject."

She looked at him anxiously. "And you can truly say you haven't had any second thoughts?"

"The only second thoughts I've had are about my not-so-bright decision to let you have your year in the city." He smiled laconically. "I don't make many mistakes, but I'm beginning to wonder if that one wasn't a major tactical error."

A burst of frustrated anger swept through Devon. She turned back to the counter and began combining the peanut butter with soy sauce and sherry. "All right, Garth, I'll be honest with you. I've had a lot of second thoughts about our plans. I know I gave you my word a year ago, but you have to admit you were putting a lot of pressure on me at the time."

"As I remember, I was making love to you at the time. You call that putting pressure on you?"

"Yes, damn it, I do!"

He didn't bother to acknowledge the fierce comment. Instead, Garth glanced around the kitchen and out into the living room. "We've got a hell of a lot of packing to do here. If we get busy after dinner tonight we should be able to get most of your personal stuff into boxes. We'll call a mover for the rest."

"Garth, please, listen to me. I really have been thinking about this and I don't believe I'm going to make you a good wife. You need someone different, someone who'll be content to live on a ranch, someone who won't mind eating beef every night of the week. Someone who won't object to cooking breakfast for you at five in the morning. Someone who won't mind the dirt and the smell of horses. Someone who won't mind driving a truck instead of a sports car. Someone who won't care that all the money has to go into land instead of more frivolous things. Someone who wants to give you a whole bunch of kids. *The last thing you need is someone like your ex-wife.*"

There was an endless moment of shattering silence and then Devon felt Garth move up behind her. He closed his big hands around her shoulders, turning her to face him. His gray eyes were gleaming as he looked down into her earnest, wary face.

"Are you trying to tell me in your own inimitable fashion that you think you're similar to my ex-wife?"

Devon curled and uncurled her fingers into her palms. "I think it's a possibility you should consider." She had never met Garth's former wife. Garth had been divorced for more than a year before he'd moved to Hawk Springs. But Devon had made several shrewd guesses about the woman based on the few, clipped comments Garth had made from time to time. She imagined a bright, beautiful creature who had enjoyed the good life Garth's money could buy but not the life-style Garth chose to live.

"My ex-wife," Garth said very distinctly, "was a shallow, selfish woman who would have let her brothers go into foster homes rather than give up her own happiness to care for them. She loved to seduce a man because it gave her a feeling of power, but in bed she was as cold as ice. A manipulator. She was all promise but no substance. When the going got tough, you could count on her to be gone. She was a beautiful woman but there was no real passion behind the beauty. She was too self-centered to be able to give herself to a man, even though in the end she ran off with one she thought could give her what she wanted. I've made a few mistakes in my life, Devon. Marrying Tamara was one of them. But I learn from my mistakes and I never make the same ones twice. You have nothing in common with her and I don't ever want to hear you comparing yourself to her again. Understood?"

Devon sucked in her breath, momentarily horrified by the thought of Garth being tied to such a woman. He deserved so much more than that. She put her hands up to frame his hard face. "I didn't realize," Devon whispered. "I thought things hadn't worked out between you and your ex-wife because she just couldn't adapt to your lifestyle. I didn't understand that she'd hurt you so much."

"She made my life hell. I was getting ready to file for divorce when she obligingly walked out. But she didn't hurt me so much as teach me a lesson. This time around I'm choosing a woman who knows how to give a man the important things. A silk shirt and a pair of silly designer jeans don't change you, honey. Underneath, you're still my sweet, honest Devon and you're the woman I'm going to marry. You grew up on a farm. You know what the lifestyle involves. You know how to make a commitment and stick to it. When you give your word, you stand by it. I'll be able to count on you no matter what happens. After

running free for a year you may need a little time to remember you belong to me, but you'll settle down when I
get you back to Hawk Springs.''

"And if I don't settle down in Hawk Springs?" Devon
prodded desperately.

"You will," he stated calmly and then he wrapped his
hand around the nape of her neck and kissed her.

Devon tried to hold back, tried to make the kiss light
and casual, a gesture of affection and friendship. But
Garth's mouth overwhelmed hers, just as it had that night
a year ago. Her lips parted beneath the probing pressure
and in another moment he was subjecting her to an intimate invasion. His tongue explored her with an aching
need and possessiveness that told its own story. Garth had
been waiting a long time. She felt the leashed hunger in
him and her own reaction was instantaneous and explo-
sive. When he took her in his arms she couldn't pretend
that what she felt for him was anything short of love. She
trembled in his hold and knew he was vitally aware of her
response.

"My God, it's been a long year, Devon." The words
were pulled from somewhere deep inside him.

For a year Devon had tried to forget the effect he had on
her, sensing the trap behind the beguiling sensuality. She
knew now the effort had been useless. Still, she struggled
to reason logically. "Marriage is so . . . so final, Garth."

"You're still afraid, aren't you?" He lifted his head,
studying her with a searching gaze. "A year ago I let you
go because I knew you needed some time to yourself, time
to be free. You'd been trapped for years by your sense of
commitment and love for your brothers. You gave up
everything for them, including a social life. I knew you
were afraid of marrying me because you were terrified
you'd find yourself in another kind of cage. You weren't

ready for it. But you've had a year, Devon. That's all the time I can give you. I'd go out of my mind if I had to wait any longer.''

"Garth . . ."

He released her. "Your noodles are about to boil over."

That was Garth, Devon thought as she turned back to the stove. Even in the midst of an emotional confrontation, he never lost sight of the practical side of life.

Devon felt desperate, torn between what she was afraid might be love and a deep wariness of what she would be getting into if she followed through on her commitment to this man. The mere thought of moving back to Hawk Springs had a stifling effect on her mind. She experienced a subtle panic that made her nervous and uneasy.

It wasn't just the thought of returning to the small town that was threatening, although that was bad enough. It was the knowledge that this time around she would be Garth's wife that really worried her. It was possible she loved him. Right now she didn't want to explore that too closely. She knew for certain she respected him and she couldn't deny the passion he drew from her, but that didn't change the fact that Saxon would be a difficult man to live with.

He would be possessive, arrogantly sure of himself, rigid and unbending when it came to the more frivolous things in life. He worked hard and demanded that others do the same. Devon was convinced that one of the reasons he wanted to marry her was that she'd proved she wasn't afraid of hard work. He wouldn't want a flighty butterfly for a wife. He needed a sturdy, practical, pragmatic, uncomplaining and undemanding farm woman. Someone with whom he could work shoulder to shoulder for the next fifty or sixty years. He didn't need a woman who'd learned to love freedom and silk. He didn't need a woman who'd learned to have fun.

"What happened to your photography this year, Devon?" Garth asked as he watched her finish dinner preparations. "Back in Hawk Springs you always had some of your photographs hanging on the walls."

"I've been doing some free-lance work. Not much." No sense explaining that she'd been just beginning to make the free-lance work pay and hoped to eventually make a career out of it.

He nodded. "You'll be able to get back into it when you return to Hawk Springs. I'm going to need some good portraits of Royal Standard and High Flyer for this year's ads in the horse magazines. I've been waiting until you got back rather than hire a photographer. I did that after you left last year and the photos weren't nearly as good as the ones you did the year before."

Devon couldn't deny the little wave of pleasure that went through her at the compliment. Royal Standard and High Flyer were two of Garth's prize Arab stallions. They commanded high stud fees. When their equine services were advertised in the horse magazines a photo was usually run along with the full-page color ad that detailed their fancy pedigrees.

The year before she'd left Hawk Springs Garth had hired Devon to take some shots of his stallions, even though she'd never had a photo published. She'd always thought of her photography as just a hobby. At the time she'd worried that Garth was merely finding a discreet way of giving her money, but she'd been reassured when the response to the ad had been very positive. It had given her the confidence to actually consider trying to make photography pay. Something else for which she owed Garth, Devon thought with an inner wince.

"I think we're ready to eat," Devon said in a subdued voice as she folded the peanut sauce into the noodles.

"Good. I've been hungry since I stopped at a fast food restaurant on the Interstate around noon. That junk food doesn't stick with you." Garth ambled over to the kitchen table, eyeing the noodle dish. "What is that, exactly?"

"Well, it's not beef," she assured him.

"I can see that. Has it got a name?"

"Don't look so skeptical. It's just noodles and vegetables in peanut sauce. Close your eyes and pretend it's a chunk of pot roast or a piece of steak." She set the dish down on the table and sorted out the tableware. Garth slid onto the seat across from her.

"I'm hungry enough to eat anything." He watched her ladle out a hearty serving and set it in front of him. He tried the mixture rather cautiously, chewing reflectively.

"Well?" Devon demanded.

"It's not bad. A little strange, but not bad." Garth took a much bigger second bite. "I think I can get through it without having to close my eyes."

"You don't know how relieved I am," Devon said dryly.

"Is this the kind of thing you like to cook these days?"

"Afraid so. I make a heck of a pasta primavera, too."

"I won't even ask what that is."

"Smart man," she said with an approving smile. Across the table his gaze met hers, and for a moment a silent, humorous communication took place that left Devon feeling suddenly very nervous. "Garth?"

"What?" Garth was busy forking up another bite of noodles.

"Did you have any *fun* this year?" For the life of her she didn't know what gave her the courage to ask him the same question he'd asked her earlier when they'd entered the apartment. But the words were out and Devon had to know the truth.

"No," he said simply and went back to his noodles.

Devon stared at him. "No? Garth, what I meant was have you dated? Seen anyone else?"

"What you're asking is if I've been to bed with anyone else," he said bluntly. "And the answer is no. For the same reason your answer was no. We had an understanding, didn't we, Devon?"

She was still feeling slightly stunned. "We talked about getting married in a year's time, but I certainly never expected you to...to stay celibate for all that time."

"Why not?"

Devon waved a hand weakly. "Well, you're a man and I just assumed you'd need or at least want... That is, I was sure you'd get involved with someone this past year."

Understanding abruptly lit his eyes and his mouth hardened. "You thought I'd find someone else and let you off the hook, is that it?"

"I thought you might realize that another woman might make you a better wife, Garth," Devon said with cautious dignity.

"Ah, Devon," he murmured. "What am I going to do with you? You're going to hunt for any available loophole, aren't you? Don't you know it's time to stop running?"

She couldn't take her eyes off him. "A whole year, Garth? You haven't been with another woman for a whole year?"

Garth poured the last of the wine into his glass. "I told you, it's been a long twelve months," he said calmly.

Three

———

I assume you've made plans to give the furniture away to charity?" Garth stood in the center of the black and white living room, surveying the sleek, sophisticated love seat, lacquer tables and assorted chairs. He hadn't wasted any time after dinner. As soon as the dishes were done he'd begun organizing the packing.

Devon, who had been trailing helplessly around behind him while he took inventory and gave instructions, finally dug in her heels. She loved her furniture. "Give it away? Are you crazy, Garth? This furniture is beautiful. I love it. I handpicked every piece and I'm not about to give it away. It took me weeks to make my decisions on the coffee table and the love seat. I had to wait for the chairs to be shipped from Italy."

His brows rose at the unexpected outburst. He seemed to realize this wasn't going to be the minor issue he had assumed. "Devon, this stuff isn't exactly the kind of thing we can use at Hawk's Flight. Besides, we've already got enough furniture there.''

"I've seen your furniture," she retorted, remembering the solid, uninteresting pieces that filled his home. "Early American Ordinary. Not even good examples of the type. No style and no interest."

"It was in the house when I bought the place. It's held up well for years and will probably last for another decade."

"A truly chilling thought."

"I never realized you took furniture so personally," he muttered dryly.

"I couldn't afford to take it personally until this past year when I finally had the freedom and the money to buy what I wanted."

Garth walked over to the love seat and examined a cushion. "This stuff cost a lot?"

Devon nearly choked and then her sense of humor came to her aid. "Oh, yes, Garth, it cost a lot. But that's not the worst part."

He frowned at her, letting the cushion drop back into place. "What's the worst part?"

"I'm still making payments on it," she informed him sweetly.

He looked scandalized. "Payments? On furniture? You bought it on time?"

Devon crossed her arms under her breasts and regarded him with amused defiance. She knew perfectly well Garth wouldn't think of going into debt for anything except land, and the only reason he occasionally took out loans for property was because he was businessman enough to know it made more sense than buying land outright. "I'll be finished paying for it in three months."

"I can't believe it. Why didn't you just get some stuff at yard sales or secondhand stores? Or you could have used some of the stuff you had in Hawk Springs instead of selling it before you left town. Why in hell did you go into hock for a pile of foreign furniture?'' Garth was truly dumbfounded.

Devon ambled over to the love seat and threw herself down on it. She stroked the black leather fondly. "I've told you why. It's beautiful and I love it."

He glared down at her. "You'd never have done something like this back in Hawk Springs. You were too sensible."

"True. I had other responsibilities at the time. But this past year I've been responsible for no one but myself. It's been great. I've discovered that there is a very unsensible side to my nature. You're lucky you arrived when you did," she added with mocking seriousness. "I was going to start shopping for a car next week. One of those cute little two-seater import models. Something with dash and flair. Just like my furniture."

"You're right. It's a good thing I got here when I did. I can just see something like that sitting in the drive at the ranch. About as useful as a hole in a rowboat." He shot her a glowering look and then sighed. "All right, we'll have to make arrangements for this stuff to be shipped down to Hawk Springs. I don't know what the hell we're going to do with it when it gets there. Put it into storage until we can arrange to sell it, I guess."

"Over my dead body." Devon glanced at her precious Italian furniture, feeling goaded. It was ridiculous, but the furniture was rapidly becoming a symbol of some sort. "Actually, I think it will look rather interesting in your living room."

Garth's eyes narrowed. "Over *my* dead body. It looks like it would fall apart if someone breathed on it heavily. That chair looks about as comfortable as a packing crate and there isn't any place to put your feet. Don't the Italians believe in recliners? And how's a man supposed to stretch out on that miniature sofa?"

Devon took a deep breath. "The furniture and I go together, Garth. We're part of a package."

The contest of wills was shorter-lived than Devon would have believed.

"I don't really want to make a federal case out of this, Devon," Garth said quietly.

"Neither do I. But I want my furniture."

"Why is it so important to you? Because it represents the freedom you think you've been enjoying this year? Or is it a kind of security blanket for you?"

"Maybe I just don't like having all my decisions made for me," Devon suggested softly. When he flicked her a quick, questioning glance she added with a smile, "You tend to do that, Garth. You're so accustomed to making decisions and you're so good at it that you just assume you should make them for everyone around you."

His expression was stony. "Any decisions I make for you are in your best interests, honey."

"Thank you," she murmured. "Keep in mind that any decisions I might make for you are in *your* best interests."

There were a few seconds of silence while Garth tried to absorb the alien notion of anyone making decisions for him. He clearly couldn't quite grasp the concept. Instead, he must have decided Devon was amusing herself. He smiled his slow, serious smile and reached down to tug her to her feet.

"I see that your stubborn streak hasn't changed a bit during this past year." He raised his hands and speared his fingers through her hair, his gray eyes gleaming intently. "Don't fight me every step of the way, Devon. There's no reason to. Everything's already been decided. All the important decisions were made a year ago when you said you'd marry me. You're going to come back to Hawk Springs with me and we're going to make a home together. It's what we both want."

"Do we?" she asked uncertainly.

"Yes. And I think deep inside you know it. This year apart has been a mistake in some ways. It's put doubts in your head and made you wonder about what you're doing, but you'll stop fretting when you're settled in Hawk Springs. It's where you belong, sweetheart. And Lord knows, I've waited long enough to bring you home."

"Garth?"

"Do you have any idea," he asked, his voice turning husky as he continued to wind his hands in her hair, "of how many nights I've lain awake remembering what it was like between us?"

A curious flare of excitement and hope came to life within Devon. "Did you really lie awake thinking about me?"

"More nights than I can remember. I've missed you so much, Devon. I thought this year would never end." He uttered something half under his breath and then he pulled her closer, folding his strong arms around her until she was pinned tightly and securely. "I'm not going to let you go again. I couldn't."

Devon slowly put her arms around him, letting herself relax against the welcoming strength of his body. He smelled so good, she thought fleetingly. There was a tang of honest sweat mixed with the indefinable essence of fresh air and sunshine, soap and leather. Her arms tightened as something inside her stirred in response. This was Garth,

the man who'd taught her the meaning of passion on that
fateful night a year ago. He was telling her he'd been
wanting her for a long, lonely year. She couldn't deny that
a part of her had been wanting him, too.

"You feel so good, Devon, and it's been so long. We're
nowhere near Hawk Springs. There's no one who will
know if I take you to bed tonight. You were always so
careful not to cause gossip, but no one will talk about you
after tonight. I was going to wait until after we're married
but I honestly don't think I can." His mouth hungrily
skimmed down the arch of her throat and his hands moved
on her back in a sensual, stroking motion.

Devon shivered restlessly, aware of the excitement curling to life inside her. No other man had even remotely interested her this past year and she knew now what her body
had known all along. She'd been waiting for Garth. It
would probably complicate things if she made love with
him tonight. There was so much they had to work out, so
many decisions yet to be made. Garth might be certain of
the future in his own mind, but Devon was plagued with
uncertainty and doubt.

Yet none of those uncertainties or doubts seemed an
adequate shield against the need that was beginning to
burn within her.

"Garth, the packing..."

"The packing can wait until morning," he said. "I
can't." His hands moved on her more urgently, pulling the
silk blouse free of her waistband. He sighed with satisfaction when he slid his rough fingers underneath the delicate fabric and touched her smooth skin.

Devon gave up trying to use common sense to halt the
inevitable. Garth wasn't the only one who'd been waiting
a year to rediscover the passionate side of their relationship. She'd told herself she didn't want to make a com-

mitment, that she needed her freedom after so many years of being confined by responsibilities, but it was hard to look into the future when Garth was holding her like this.

A year was a long time.

"Devon, you feel so good. Warm and silky and soft. I don't think I'll ever be able to get enough of you. Can't you tell what you do to me?"

She could feel his desire and knew a primitive joy in being able to provoke such a response. Devon gloried in the tough, muscled feel of him. She slipped her fingertips over his back, kneading with catlike sensitivity.

"Sweetheart, you're going to drive me out of my mind." Garth groaned and captured her mouth. When she parted her lips for him he shuddered and swept inside to take what she was offering.

Devon barely felt the silk blouse sliding off her shoulders as Garth found the buttons and undid them. But she was suddenly aware of coolness against her skin and then the heat of Garth's hands as he gently cupped her breasts.

When he found and released the catch of her bra, Devon sighed into his mouth. She trembled as his callused palms glided over her nipples, coaxing them into taut peaks.

"Oh, Garth, I'd almost forgotten what it was like," Devon breathed in soft wonder.

"I never even came close to forgetting," he said thickly. "The memories have been threatening to push me over the edge. Just thinking about the way you respond to me was enough to send me into a hell of a lot of cold showers this past year. And nothing's changed, has it?" He touched her taut nipple with his thumb.

Devon could hear the masculine satisfaction in his voice, but she didn't really mind just then. He was right. In this respect, nothing had changed. She shook her head in mute agreement and Garth kissed her again, deeply, longingly. Devon felt a year's worth of aching need and leashed passion in him and knew that in that moment she wanted nothing more than to release that passion and satisfy the need.

She began to fumble with the buttons of his shirt, wanting more of him. Impatiently Garth shrugged out of the garment. When Devon splayed her fingers against his chest, he covered one of her small hands briefly with his own, restraining her lightly.

"The bedroom," he muttered hoarsely. "Let's go to the bedroom."

Devon smiled mistily. "Why?" she asked, so caught up in the sensual longing that was flowing in her veins that she didn't stop to consider her question.

"Because I'll never fit on that damn little couch."

"There's plenty of room on the rug." She lifted her face shyly to meet his eyes and put her arms around his neck. Her own boldness startled her, but she didn't regret it. If she couldn't be adventuresome with Garth, she couldn't be adventuresome with anyone. He was the only man she wanted. After a year of waiting, she understood that now with blinding clarity. Deliberately she pressed her breasts against his broad, hard chest and immediately felt the exciting tickle of the dark, curling hair that grew in profusion on his tanned skin.

"Why should we use the rug when there's a perfectly good bed waiting just down the hall?" Garth asked, looking genuinely taken aback.

"I don't know. I wasn't thinking." She flushed and buried her face against his chest. She was rapidly beginning to regret her impulsive suggestion. She should have guessed Garth would have conservative ideas about appropriate behavior in this sort of situation. The one other time he had made love to her had been in her small, single bed back in Hawk Springs.

"Honey, I don't think that rug is going to be very comfortable."

"Never mind," she breathed, not wanting to spoil the moment. "I don't know what got into me. Let's go to the bedroom." Embarrassed now, she started to turn away from him.

His eyes dropped to her tip-tilted breasts and he pulled her back into his arms. "No," he declared. "We'll try the rug if that's what you want. God knows, at the moment I don't particularly care where we are. I just know I have to have you and soon or I'll come apart. I don't think you really understand what you do to me."

He eased her down onto the thick white rug, lowering himself beside her. He bent his head to kiss the small valley between her breasts and then he took a nipple into his mouth. Her momentary shyness fled beneath the loving onslaught.

Devon cried out softly and arched herself against him. She clenched her fingers into his hair as the level of her own excitement leaped several notches.

"This is what I spent so many nights remembering," Garth told her with deep satisfaction. "The way you come alive in my arms. It's like nothing I've ever known, Devon."

He flattened his palm on her stomach and the heat of it seemed to permeate her body. Then he was unfastening the tight jeans and sliding them down over her hips. The lacy, nude-toned underpants came off with the designer denim and in a matter of seconds Devon was lying naked beside Garth.

When she opened her eyes she saw him watching her and felt herself warming all over under the brilliant, possessive, raw hunger in his gaze.

"Garth?"

"I want you so badly, Devon." He kissed her lingeringly. "So badly." He tangled his fingers in the dampening curls between her thighs. "And you want me, don't you? Say it. Please, say it, Devon."

"I want you," she vowed. "More than I've ever wanted anything else in my life." Including her so-called freedom, she realized distantly.

The crucial, but fleeting thought was driven from her mind as Garth touched the secret part of her. Gently he opened her legs and found the sensitive core of her need. She knew she was growing moist and soft under his touch and the knowledge of her uninhibited response made her retreat for an instant. Her quick, sizzling reaction to Garth was a little unnerving.

"What's the matter, Devon?" He continued to stroke her, waiting for her to relax again. "Don't be afraid. I know it's been a long time but I won't hurt you. I'd never hurt you."

"I know that. It's just that you make me so... so wild. I'd forgotten how you affect me." Her clear eyes met his. "It frightens me a little, Garth."

"You'll get used to the feeling, I promise." He lowered his head again, this time to trail a string of soft, nibbling kisses down her stomach. "You taste so good. Hot and spicy."

She shivered again and clutched at his shoulders as he began to string the kisses even lower. Making love on the rug was adventurous enough for her, she realized. This kind of intimacy, even with Garth, was too much. She tried to urge him back up along the length of her body.

"Garth, please, I don't . . . I can't . . ."

But Garth ignored the stumbling protest and the sharp little nails digging into his shoulders. Instead he took his time exploring her in ways that left Devon shuddering with reaction. She soon stopped struggling and gave herself up to the exquisite sensations he was arousing within her.

Garth might have limited notions about the proper time and place for making love, but it was obvious he put no limitations whatsoever on the act itself. Devon was breathless and desperate by the time he had finished teaching her the true meaning of being adventurous.

"Please, Garth, oh, please. I can't wait any longer." She lifted herself against him, pleading now for the release only he could give her.

"Neither can I," he said thickly as he pulled away from her to unfasten his belt and slide out of his pants.

When he came back down beside her, Devon sighed and went into his embrace with all the certainty of a homing pigeon returning to its mate.

"This is where you belong, Devon. Here in my arms." Garth sprawled heavily on top of her, drinking in the warmth of her mouth as he fitted himself between her legs.

Devon felt the hard, throbbing maleness pressing close and she opened herself to take Garth deep within her. He started to enter her, felt the tightness and paused. But when she sank her nails back into his shoulders and raised her hips, he hesitated no longer.

"Devon!"

She made a small, muffled sound as he drove himself into her. For a few seconds her body felt unbearably full. Garth lay still, trembling above her, while he waited for her to adjust to him.

"It's been so long," she whispered.

"Too long." As he felt the rush of her quickly returning excitement, he began to stroke slowly and rhythmi-
cally.

Devon found the tempo and echoed it, clinging tightly
to the hard, muscled frame above her. Her mind whirled
with the force of the building crescendo.

When the finale came she wrapped herself around Garth
and called his name in a soft litany of the love she could no
longer deny.

Garth felt the tiny shivers that signaled her release, felt
the gentle way her body clenched around him and then he
heard the sound of his name on her lips. That was all it
took to pull him over the edge after her. His hoarse excla-
mation of satisfaction made Devon cling to him even more
tightly and they held on to each other as the glittering
fragments of the climax faded slowly around them.

I love him, Devon thought as she came slowly back to
reality. *I've loved him all along. What am I going to
do?*

She felt Garth stir in her arms, lifting himself on his elbows. His eyes were gleaming with a lazy satisfaction that
was all male and as old as time. Devon gave a soft, broken laugh and tried ineffectually to shake him.

"Don't look at me like that," she ordered.

"Like what?"

The question was an honest inquiry. He wasn't teasing
her, Devon realized. He was unaware of the blatant evi-
dence of his own masculine contentment and possessiveness. It radiated from him like an aura but he wouldn't
know that. "Never mind," she whispered, not knowing
how to put her rebuke into words. How did you tell a man
to stop looking like a conquering hero?

"Devon?"

"Hmm?"

"Are you finally through running from me? Will you stop fighting me now and come home where you belong?"

Some of her sweet lassitude began to evaporate under the intensity of his gaze. There was no point looking for loopholes and she knew it. Still, she felt obliged to point out the obvious before she finally gave in to the inevitable.

"It won't be easy, Garth. Do you realize that? We're different, you and I. I can't give you my word that I'm going to be able to be the kind of wife you want."

He stopped her gentle warning with his mouth. When he lifted his head again he was smiling faintly. "You are exactly the kind of wife I want."

"I've changed, Garth," she told him earnestly. "You knew a different version of me when I lived in Hawk Springs."

"You couldn't possibly change so much that I'd no longer want you."

She shook her head. "I'm not so sure about that. You like the traditional, practical things in life and you take them so seriously. Meat and potatoes at dinner and four-wheel-drive vehicles. When was the last time you had a party or took a vacation? Have you ever gone to Hawaii and sat on a beach and done absolutely nothing? Have you ever bought a pair of sexy black briefs for yourself?"

His eyes widened and some of the lazy satisfaction went out of him. "Devon, you're not making much sense. There's no point trying to convince me we're not going to make it together, because I know we are. Stop looking for an exit, honey. There isn't one.''

Devon let out her breath and closed her eyes. ''I hope you know what we're doing.''

''I usually do,'' he reminded her with totally unconscious arrogance. Then he kissed her again and rolled reluctantly off of her. ''Good Lord, we've got a lot of packing to do.''

Devon's wistful mood vanished in the face of yet another example of Garth's boundless pragmatism. Trust him to start worrying about something as mundane as packing right after he'd finished making shattering love to her.

One last possible way to avoid the unavoidable leaped into Devon's brain. She voiced it before giving herself a chance to think about the consequences. ''There's one alternative to marriage that we haven't considered,'' she said quickly.

He sat up, running his fingers through his hair before reaching for his pants. ''What's that?'' He didn't seem particularly interested.

Devon gathered her courage and plunged in with her suggestion. ''We could try things out between us, Garth.''

He swept a glance down the length of her, his mouth tilting slightly in amusement. ''We've already tried things out twice and they work better each time. I'm looking forward to trying them out again as soon as I get a ring on your finger.''

''That's not what I meant.''

''What did you mean?''

Devon bit her lip and then said baldly, ''I'm suggesting we have an affair before we get married.''

He was halfway to his feet. His head came around, an astounded expression on his face. "You're suggesting *what*?"

"You heard me," she said mutinously. "I think we should become lovers. Get to know each other before we make the commitment of marriage. Marriage is a big step, Garth. You, of all people know that. Surely you don't want to make another mistake?"

"Lovers? You want to have an affair? In Hawk Springs?" He was on his feet now, but he seemed to have forgotten his pants. He stood in front of her, towering over her with his feet braced slightly apart, his hands on his hips. He seemed totally unaware of his own magnificent nudity. His eyes had gone very cold and very cloudy and there was a savage tightness around his mouth. Garth's gathering anger was a storm about to burst. "You're suggesting I take you back to Hawk Springs as my mistress? Are you out of your mind? *Hawk Springs?* People in Hawk Springs don't have mistresses. They have sleazy one-night stands that both parties regret the next day and that the whole town talks about, or else they get married. There's no in-between in a small town. And you damn well know it."

"I wasn't suggesting I go back with you. I could stay here." Devon clutched at her emerald silk shirt, feeling woefully unprepared to face the cataclysm. She was already wishing she'd kept her mouth shut. The easy, satisfied mood that had descended on Garth immediately following the lovemaking had vanished, leaving behind a very angry man. She should have guessed Garth's reaction.

"Oh sure. You stay here where you can run free all week
long in the city and I'm supposed to spend most of my
weekend driving the interstate so I can spend Saturday
night with you? Don't be an idiot, Devon. Don't you think
everyone in Hawk Springs is going to figure out what's
going on?"

"Is that all you care about? What the people in town say
about you?" she flared, feeling pressured. "I'd have
thought you wouldn't give a damn."

"I don't give a damn what anyone says about me," he
exploded. "I'm trying to protect you. Can't you get that
through your head?"

"I don't care what anyone back in Hawk Springs says
about me!"

"Well, I sure as hell do. And even if I didn't, I wouldn't
tolerate the kind of situation you're suggesting. I'm a
working man, Devon. I don't have time for fancy playthings and that's what mistresses are. I want a wife. A
partner. A companion and a lover. I want someone I can
talk to over breakfast. A woman who can keep my bed
warm at night. I want a woman who understands ranching, someone who won't expect me to perform like a sexual athlete after I've spent sixteen hours delivering foals.
Someone who won't expect me to entertain her. I don't
have time for toys, regardless of how good they are in bed.
Is that clear?"

"Very clear." Devon knew she was flushing all the way
down to her breasts. It had been a stupid idea. A last-ditch
tactic that she should have known would be useless. She
would have given anything to retract the whole thing. She
scrambled to her feet, pulling on her panties and draping
the blouse around herself in a precarious fashion. "Ex-

'cuse me. I'm going to take a shower.'' She turned toward the hallway, intent on fleeing.

She didn't get far. Garth put out a hand and clamped it very firmly around her wrist. He didn't use any force but Devon was halted as effectively as if she'd reached the end of a rope. Slowly she turned to face him.

"You promised to marry me, Devon."

"Yes."

"I don't want a mistress. I don't want a part-time lover. I want a wife."

"Yes." Garth always knew what he wanted, Devon thought. He didn't mince words or offer compromises. He didn't have time for toys and playthings and games.

"Be honest with yourself, Devon. You want me as much as I want you."

"Yes."

His expression softened. "It's time to stop testing the end of the rope, honey. I've already given you all I'm going to allow. Hell, I've given you all I can without driving myself nuts. You've had your year and now it's time to come home. You're acting like a skittish filly who doesn't have any good reason to be afraid but who insists on fighting the bridle anyway."

"You have such a way with words, Garth." Devon wrinkled her nose in chagrin as the last of her resistance gave way. "You could have found a better metaphor."

"I know horses. I don't know metaphors." He tugged her slowly toward him and brushed his mouth across hers. "I also know you, Devon. And you know me. It's going to work out between us. Can't you trust me, honey?"

Of course she could trust him. This was Garth, whose word was good until hell froze over. That wasn't the point,

Devon thought in resignation. But she didn't seem to be able to find any other logical points to use in the argument, so she did what most people and horses did around Garth Saxon.

She yielded to the inevitable.

Four

If it had been anyone other than Garth Saxon organizing the packing of her possessions, Devon knew she would have been amazed and astounded. But she was familiar with the quiet, calm, deliberate manner in which Garth worked, and it was really no surprise when he announced they were ready to leave shortly after noon the following day.

"That's it, then," Garth said as he loaded the last box into the pickup. "Your landlady has the key and she'll let the movers in tomorrow. They'll handle the books, kitchen stuff and that damn silly furniture. We've got everything else. Let's get going. With any luck we'll be home in time for dinner."

Devon thought of the large roast, the overcooked vegetables and the heavy pie that would probably be waiting. "Is Beverly Middleton still your housekeeper?"

"Sure." Garth cinched down the load in the back of the pickup. "She was working for the previous owners when I bought Hawk's Flight. Knows the place from one end to the other. Why would I change housekeepers?"

"Why indeed," Devon murmured as she walked back up the stairs to take one last look around the neat little flat that had been her home for a year. Bev Middleton had cooked and cleaned for the elderly couple who had owned the stud farm before Garth bought it. She was a good-hearted, friendly woman, but short on imagination, especially when it came to food. Garth had been quite content to have her stay on and manage his house for him. Her style suited him perfectly. Garth saw no reason to change things that already seemed to work. "If it ain't broke, don't fix it," was one of his mottoes.

Feeling strangely ambivalent Devon walked through her apartment, checking drawers and opening closet doors. Garth stood in the doorway and watched, his expression remote and unreadable.

"It's time to go, Devon," he said quietly.

"I know." She stood at the graceful bay window, her fingers stuffed into the back pockets of her designer jeans. "It's such a pretty little apartment, Garth. I've been so comfortable here. It was the first place that was all mine."

He hesitated and then moved to stand behind her. "You won't miss it when you've been back in Hawk Springs for a while." He put his hands on her shoulders and dropped a small kiss into her hair.

Devon felt the gruff gentleness in him and knew that Garth wasn't insensitive to her feelings at that moment. In his own way he was trying to reassure her that she was making the right decision. After all, she told herself ruefully, it was *his* decision and his decisions were almost always right.

That thought amused her and the uncertainty she had been feeling vanished. The truth was, going back to Hawk Springs was her decision, too. She had made it a year ago, and last night it had been reinforced when she had finally acknowledged the reality of her love for Garth. She turned around with a decisive movement.

"We'd better get going if we're to be in Hawk Springs in time for dinner."

"Yes," he agreed, studying her assessingly, "we'd better move."

Garth watched her stride across the white carpet and something inside him tightened. With her new, deceptively casual hairstyle, expensive jeans, blouse with padded shoulders and tiny, strappy leather sandals she looked very trendy. She had adapted well to her new life-style. It worried him that she'd been able to do it so easily.

He had been so sure that she would miss Hawk Springs within a few weeks or months. He knew he'd hoped that she would decide she'd make a mistake and come rushing back to familiar territory, back to his waiting arms. Instead, she'd settled right into a life-style that should have been totally alien to her. The two and a half years she'd spent in Los Angeles while in college had probably prepared her to make the transition to the city again last year. Apparently she'd had no trouble at all learning big-city ways.

Not all big-city ways, though, Garth thought with deep thankfulness as he followed Devon downstairs to the truck. Some part of her had known she belonged to him. There had been no other men. She'd acknowledged that and he believed her. Devon didn't have it in her to lie. One of the reasons he wanted her so badly was that he knew he could trust her. Trust ranked very high on his list of priorities in a wife. It was number one.

Even if she hadn't admitted the fact that there had been no other men, he would have known the truth last night when he made love to her. The shy, gentle passion and the pent-up hunger he'd released told him all he'd needed to know. Devon hadn't spent the past year gaining sexual experience.

Garth's mood lightened at the thought. She'd waited for him because deep down she'd realized she wanted him and not some fancy city dude who drove a Porsche and wore a designer tie. On some level Devon understood that, even if she was dragging her feet about going back to Hawk Springs.

Reassured, Garth opened the truck door for Devon, who raised her eyebrows in mild amusement at the courtesy. She said nothing, however, and Garth walked around to the driver's side, keys in hand.

When he pulled away from the curb he saw Devon glance back once more but she didn't comment. Relieved to be on the road at last, Garth gave his attention to making his way through the city traffic.

"I figure we can arrange the wedding for next Saturday," he said easily as he found the freeway entrance ramp. "That way Lee and Kurt will be able to get away to attend. I'm sure you'll want them there. I'll call Ryan and tell him he's invited. We'll keep it small and simple. Bev can fix lunch afterward. That should do it. I'll be able to take the weekend off unless this buyer I've been talking to recently decides to show up to take a look at a couple of colts I'm going to sell to him. You know how it goes with buyers. But if McShaney decides to land on our doorstep next weekend, we'll take off the following weekend. Won't make that much difference."

"Take off where?" Devon asked far too politely.

Garth didn't like the tone of her voice. What was bothering her now? "Oh, I don't know. Maybe the coast. Would you like to spend your honeymoon on the coast?"

"Depends. How long is this honeymoon going to last?"

Garth frowned. "I told you. I'll take the weekend off."

"That's not a very long honeymoon."

Some of the relief he'd been feeling since he'd closed the door for the last time on Devon's apartment began to dissipate. It seemed as though every time he thought he'd gotten something settled with Devon, she threw a wrench into the gears. "Devon, I told you, I'm negotiating with a potential buyer. The deal's been in the works for a couple of months. In addition to that, I'm selling some property down in Arizona. That deal's been simmering for quite a while too. It should close any day now and I don't want to be out of touch too long until it's signed, sealed and delivered. On top of that, I'm having a new barn built and I have to be on hand to supervise. No telling what that contractor will do if he thinks I'm not looking over his shoulder. Besides, you know damn well Hawk's Flight doesn't run itself. I can't just take off for days at a time."

"Why the coast?" she asked unexpectedly.

Garth felt a prickle of unease. "I thought you'd like a weekend on the coast. You always said you like the ocean."

"Where on the coast, exactly, Garth?" she prodded softly.

"Does it matter? There's some nice country around Santa Barbara."

"Nice country? Are you by any chance thinking of buying some land near Santa Barbara? Or looking at some horses, perhaps?"

Garth's sense of unease grew. "Might as well kill two birds with one stone, honey. The Santa Barbara area would be a nice spot for a honeymoon and there is a piece of land near there I've been thinking about picking up. Someone I know has a good colt for sale down there, too. I thought we'd have a look at it while we're in the area. Doesn't that seem reasonable?''

"You're going to spend my honeymoon buying property and horses?''

"I told you," he said earnestly, "there's no reason we can't kill two birds with one stone.''

"Let's get one thing clear, Garth Saxon. I do not intend to kill any birds on my honeymoon. I don't like the sound of your wedding plans. I'm going to scrap all of them, from Bev Middleton's lunch to the honeymoon.''

Garth felt himself grow suddenly, searingly cold. He realized he was gripping the wheel of the pickup as though it were a life preserver. He'd been so certain it was finally settled between them. "Devon, what the hell's the matter with you? I thought we'd worked this out. You know you're going to marry me.''

"If marriage is what you want, Garth, marriage is what you'll get. But we'll do it my way.''

He snapped a forbidding glance at her and discovered her soft mouth was set in a very firm line. "What, precisely, do you mean by your way?'' he asked evenly.

"Well, for starters, I don't like the sound of a quickie wedding with only a few close relatives in attendance. Tacky. And the thought of Bev Middleton cooking up a mess of gray-green beans and roast beef for the wedding lunch is enough to make me nauseated in advance. I like Bev, but I don't care for her cooking. And last but by no means least, I have no interest in a weekend honeymoon on the coast, where I'll get to amuse myself trailing around after you watching you look at land or horses.''

"But, Devon..."

"I'll take over the planning of the wedding. And I'll need at least a month."

"A *month*!"

"That's right. I'll need that long to get out the invitations and plan the menu for the reception. I am not having green beans and beef at my wedding party."

"Devon, this is getting ridiculous."

"It gets better," she promised him. "I think we'll go to Hawaii for our honeymoon."

"*Hawaii*?"

"Don't worry, we might be able to find a ranch on Hawaii for you to look at. We'll also find volcanoes and beaches and palm trees and luxury hotels. We'll be a few thousand miles from Hawk Springs and you won't be able to concentrate on anything except us."

"Devon, I told you, I can't just take off like that."

"Of course you can. You're just not used to the idea of taking a real vacation."

"Honey, be reasonable," he pleaded, "If we do things my way they'll be a whole lot simpler."

"They'll also be a whole lot less interesting. I want a big wedding celebration and a real honeymoon. Don't worry, Garth, I'll handle everything. You won't have to do a thing except show up on time."

She was serious, he realized. Devon was dead set on making a big production out of an event he had always assumed could be handled with the minimum of fuss and disruption. This past year had caused enough disruption in his life, as far as he was concerned. All he wanted to do now was get Devon legally bound to him and settled in at the ranch so that they could get on with their lives.

Now, here she was, making things difficult.

But at least she wasn't trying to wriggle out of the marriage altogether, he reminded himself. With that realization, Garth was aware of a giant wave of relief washing over him. For a few minutes there, he'd thought she was about to tell him she'd changed her mind about marrying him altogether. He'd been terribly afraid her inner uncertainty had gotten the best of her desire for him. Garth had been aware of the tightrope he was walking from the moment he'd arrived in San Francisco and found her looking so sophisticated and at ease in that singles bar. He could only be grateful that the latest stumbling block she'd placed in his path was relatively small.

"You're sure you want to go through all the hassle of a big wedding and a trip to Hawaii?" he asked finally.

Devon heard the resigned acceptance in his voice and smiled to herself. Already she was feeling much better. The trick to dealing with Garth was to be firm and assertive, she decided. Start out as you mean to continue. "I don't mind in the least," she assured him blithely. "It will be fun to plan everything."

"Sounds more like a waste of time to me."

He wasn't going to fight her, Devon thought happily. He was going to let her do this her way. "Don't worry, Garth, I won't bother you with any of the details. Just arrange your schedule so that you'll have a week off next month."

"A whole week?"

"Don't look so stricken. It'll be good for you." The man had a lot to learn, Devon decided. He needed to learn that there was more to life than running a ranch and shouldering responsibilities. He needed to learn that there was a place in life for the frivolous and the nonserious. He needed to learn to relax and enjoy himself. He needed to learn there was something else out there to eat besides beef. He needed to learn that marriage could be playful as well as passionate, that a relationship could be fun as well as a serious partnership.

He needed to learn to lighten up a little so that he could learn to love.

She'd better find a way to get the lesson across, because she loved him and she was about to tie herself to this man for life.

It was a sobering thought. Some of Devon's cheerful determination faded later that day as the rich lands of California's fertile Central Valley came into view. Small sleepy farm towns that reminded her of Hawk Springs and acres of lush fields slipped past the windows of the truck. When you drove through this part of California it was difficult to remember the state's glitzy media image.

Here in the inner heart of California there was no sign of the glitter of Hollywood, the glamour of the Malibu beachfront, the sophistication of San Francisco or the picturesque vineyards of the northern wine country. This was farm and ranch country. The small towns shared the vices, virtues and love of gossip that characterized small towns everywhere.

"What are you smiling about, Devon?" Garth asked after a long period of silence.

She leaned her elbow on the window edge and rested her head against her hand. "I was just thinking about my big plan for us to have an affair. You were right. It would have shocked the socks off Hawk Springs."

"You can say that again."

"Might have been fun to make everyone sit up and goggle, though," she mused. "When I think of all the years I had to be so careful not to cause gossip in case it got back to Lee and Kurt and hurt them . . ." She let the sentence trail off.

"You think it might be humorous to get even now by doing something outrageous?" Garth shook his head, but he was smiling faintly. "I think I can understand the feeling."

That surprised her. "You can?"

"Sure. But I'd just as soon you resisted the temptation," he added wryly. "We're going to have to live there, remember? I guess towns as tiny and remote as Hawk Springs have their drawbacks but there are advantages, too."

"I know," Devon admitted. "Why do you think I decided to stay there with Lee and Kurt after our parents were killed? I thought about taking what was left from the sale of the farm and moving to L.A. or Sacramento or some other city, but I decided it would be safer to let the boys finish growing up in a small town and a familiar environment. I'd already spent enough time in L.A. to know what can happen to a kid there. I didn't know if I'd be able to keep Lee off the street. He was so wild during those last couple of years of high school."

"You had a lot on your hands."

"I owe you a lot for the help you gave me during his senior year," Devon said reflectively. "I was at my wit's end. He was threatening to quit school and leave town. Then there were the speeding tickets and the nights he came home drunk." She closed her eyes, remembering. "God, I was scared, Garth."

"It's over, Devon. Lee's going to be okay. You saw him at Christmas. He's happy in college and he's got his feet on the ground."

"Thanks to you. That night the sheriff called at three in the morning to tell me he had Lee in custody, I nearly went out of my mind."

"Instead, you called me."

"Yes," Devon said softly. "Instead, I called you."

"It was the first and only time you'd ever asked for my help," he said.

Devon chuckled, able to laugh about it now. "Well, you've got to admit, the first and only time was a major event. I was hardly asking for a small favor." In desperation she had finally turned to the man who had been offering friendship and more for over a year.

She had been wary of accepting what Garth was offering, so certain that soon she would finally be free of Hawk Springs and all her obligations, so convinced she hadn't wanted to tie herself to a man who was, in turn, tied to his land and his horses. One more year, she'd told herself over and over again during Lee's senior year in high school. One more year and she would be free.

But the night the sheriff had called, she'd known she couldn't handle Lee alone. She'd needed help and she'd known where she could get it. It was Garth who'd dealt with the sheriff. It was Garth who'd calmly taken charge of Devon's rebellious and resentful brother. And in doing so, he'd taken a great weight off Devon's shoulders. When it came to the crunch, Garth would always be there, Devon thought. A rock to lean on.

How did you teach a rock to enjoy the lighter side of life and love?

"Doesn't look like much has changed in Hawk Springs since I left," Devon remarked as Garth exited the interstate and drove into town. In truth, she would have been startled if anything *had* changed. Devon was certain the small assortment of shops on Main Street looked exactly as they must have looked twenty, thirty, maybe forty years previously. She knew the styles featured in the windows of Perkins Clothing store were at least that far out of date.

"There's a new supermarket on the other side of town and a new restaurant on Main," Garth told her.

"It's a wonder the place survived the excitement of a new grocery store and a restaurant. Must have caused quite a sensation when they opened. What does the restaurant serve?"

"Steaks, mostly."

"Somehow, that doesn't surprise me."

"How long is it going to take to run through your repertoire of sarcastic comments on Hawk Springs?" Garth sounded mildly curious.

Devon flushed with unexpected embarrassment. "I'll try to restrain myself."

"This is your home, Devon. You were happy here once."

"That was back when I was a little girl and didn't know any better."

"Back before you started thinking of the place as a trap. You can be happy here again if you'll just give yourself a chance," Garth said seriously.

It wasn't going to be that easy, Devon thought, but Garth was the only man on the face of the earth who could make the effort worthwhile. Devon wondered if he knew that.

Hawk's Flight looked as lush and prosperous as it had the day Devon had left town. Bathed in the early-evening light from a slowly setting sun, the green pastures, pristine white fences and well-tended barns were the perfect image of rural beauty. There were several sleek mares in the fields with their foals. Garth's two magnificent stallions, High Flyer and Royal Standard were in their paddocks.

The main house also appeared very much the same, except for a fresh coat of paint. It was a low, rambling structure with plenty of old-fashioned porches and a circling drive in front. Garth had done little to it except keep it painted and in good repair since he'd bought it. He believed in maintaining buildings and equipment in good condition. But Devon knew inside the house she would find the same heavy old drapes, the same dull carpet and the same sturdy, oversize furniture that had been in the place when the former owners sold out to Garth.

Devon was examining her new home with mixed feelings when she spotted the candy-red sports car in the drive. The vehicle looked totally out of place.

"Looks like you've got visitors, Garth."

He, too, was eyeing the dashing little car. "Ryan must be here."

"Ryan? He's driving a car like that these days?"

"Says it goes with his image as an account executive. He wanted a Porsche but had to settle for the Ford when I wouldn't come across with a loan."

"Poor Ryan." Devon could just imagine that scene. It would have taken a lot of nerve for Ryan to ask his half brother for a loan for a car. Devon could have told him the courage was wasted. Garth would go to the ends of the earth for Ryan if he'd thought his brother really needed the help. But he'd draw the line at providing money for something as frivolous as a sports car. It was Garth's considered opinion that Ryan lacked common sense and judgment.

Of course, Devon reminded herself as she jumped out of the pickup, Garth probably thought she was lacking in both qualities also.

As soon as her feet hit the ground she was almost bowled over by the three huge ranch dogs that came racing around the corner of the house. They barked joyously as they greeted their master and his guest.

"I wonder what Ryan's doing here at Hawk's Flight," Garth remarked as he unloaded suitcases from the back of the pickup. "Probably wants something. But as long as he's here, he might as well make himself useful. Go inside and tell him to come out and give me a hand with this load."

"I'm sure he'll offer to help as soon as he knows we're here," Devon said pointedly. She patted one of the dogs on the head. The beast grinned delightedly, his tongue hanging out of his mouth. "There's no need to order him to give you a hand."

Garth cocked one brow in a sardonic, but silent comment and lifted another box out of the pickup. Devon started up the walk toward the front door. The dogs danced around her.

The door opened before she could knock. Beverly Middleton, in all her plump glory, stood on the threshold. Bev was in her late fifties and had been widowed for nearly ten years, and seeing her again after a year's absence, Devon was inclined to forgive the older woman's lack of imagination when it came to cooking.

"Hi, Bev. It's been awhile." It was amazing how much pleasure she felt in seeing a familiar face, Devon thought suddenly. She would never have guessed she'd miss anyone in Hawk Springs.

"Well, well, well. So he brought you back, did he?" Bev shook her head in mock wonder. "I told him when he left he'd have a job on his hands dragging you away from the big city." She came down the steps and enveloped Devon in a huge, bosomy hug. "Could have sworn you'd put up more of a fight. You were always as stubborn and proud as one of Garth's fancy, high-bred horses."

"We all know what happens to his horses," Devon murmured.

Bev laughed, stepping back again. "In the end he always has 'em eating out of the palm of his hand, doesn't he? Same way with you?"

"Not quite. But I've decided to wage my battle on his turf. How have you been, Bev? You look good."

"Can't complain," Bev said equably. "You sure look good. You've done somethin' real nice with your hair, haven't you? I like it. And where'd you get those slick jeans?"

"From a store on Union Square. They cost a fortune and Garth's been making rude comments about them since he saw them."

Before Bev could respond, Garth interrupted. "Send Ryan out here," he called from the drive. "You two can catch up on the news later. I want to get this stuff unloaded."

A thin, sandy-haired man with an open smile and amused blue eyes appeared in the doorway behind Bev. He was dressed in a European-cut shirt and a pair of men's designer jeans. "I hear you, Garth. I'm coming." Ryan came down the steps and stopped for a moment in front of Devon. He grinned. "Well, look who's here. Couldn't resist the fleshpots and temptations of Hawk Springs any longer, huh, Devon?"

"The bright lights called and here I am," she agreed blandly. "How have you been, Ryan?"

"Great. It's been a good year in L.A. Did Garth tell you I've been working there?"

"He mentioned it."

Garth interrupted again. "Are you going to stand there chatting all night or are you going to give me a hand with these things, Ryan?"

"Do I have a choice?" Ryan asked irrepressibly.

"No, you do not have a choice. Move."

"Yes, sir." Ryan gave a mock salute and brushed past Devon. "Love your jeans," he murmured as he went by her.

She laughed softly. "Yours look pretty good, too. Italian?"

"French."

"Ah."

Garth was halfway up the walk. Unceremoniously he shoved a suitcase into Ryan's hand. "You two can compare jeans some other time. I'm hungry."

"Okay," Ryan said good-naturedly. "Where do you want all this stuff?"

"The suitcases go in the south bedroom. The boxes go into the storage locker on the back porch."

Ryan started up the steps with the suitcase. "South bedroom, hmm?" He leered in a friendly fashion. "That's on the opposite side of the house from your room, Garth. Quite a walk."

Garth's expression would have frozen hellfire. "That's where Devon will be sleeping until we're married. Bev will be staying in the center bedroom and you, as long as you're here, will have the one next to mine."

Ryan glanced at Bev Middleton. "Looks like you and me get to play chaperon, Bev."

"Now, Ryan, you know perfectly well Garth wouldn't have her in the house alone with him until they're married," Bev said chidingly. "I've agreed to say here until the knot is tied." But there was a distinct twinkle in her eye when she glanced at Devon. "When it comes to Devon, the man's got a sense of propriety that would make a preacher nervous. Come on inside, Devon. You can help me get dinner on the table. Got a nice roast in the oven."

"Wonderful," Devon said under her breath.

She was unaware Garth had overheard her until he came right up behind her and drawled in her ear, "You can't have noodles and peanut butter every night. The stuff sticks to the roof of your mouth."

Devon tried to quell him with a quick glare and failed miserably. She abandoned the attempt and followed Bev Middleton into the house.

Dinner was everything Devon had been expecting. Roast beef, potatoes and thick gravy, overcooked vegetables and a huge apple pie Devon knew had been baked in her honor. It wasn't a bad meal, she told herself consolingly, if one overlooked the overcooked veggies and the high-cholesterol gravy. It was just that it was so predictable.

She was industriously sawing off another chunk of beef and listening to Garth talk about a new stallion he was considering buying when she glanced up and caught Ryan's eyes. His blue gaze was full of laughter as he watched her plow through the heavy food.

"So, tell me," Ryan said smoothly to Devon as Garth finished talking, "how was life in the big city?"

"I was about to ask you the same question," she retorted, smiling. "Garth says you're an account executive?"

"That's what I've been doing until recently." Ryan nodded enthusiastically. "My firm markets computers to small businesses. It's a hot field. Very competitive. We're putting computers into every kind of business these days."

"What do you mean, it's what you've been doing until recently?" Garth asked ominously.

Ryan's enthusiasm was replaced by a kind of grim determination that was vaguely reminiscent of his older brother. "Well, the fact is, I quit my job last week so that I could concentrate full-time on another project."

"What other project?" Garth asked much too softly.

Ryan cleared his throat. "Similar line of work, but I'll be my own boss."

There was an uncomfortable silence at the table. Devon hastened to fill it. "I'll bet Garth could use a computer to help run this ranch and keep track of all his real estate investments."

Garth's head came up abruptly. "When hell freezes over. You don't raise horses with computers."

Ryan's mouth thinned briefly but he kept his attention on Devon. "A friend of mine and I are planning to open our own business."

"Selling computers?" Devon asked with interest.

"That's right." Ryan shot a challenging glance toward Garth, who was surveying his half brother with an assessing expression. "It would take some capital to get started, naturally. But Phil and I both know what we're doing." As he spoke Ryan's voice again picked up enthusiasm. "We've both had experience in the field and between us we've made some good contacts. They'd be the basis of our new client list."

"I think," Garth said evenly, "I'm beginning to understand why I came home to find you on my doorstep this evening. You wouldn't by any chance be shopping for cash to put into this new business venture of yours, would you?"

Ryan took a deep breath. "I'd like to talk to you about the possibilities, Garth. And I'd like for you to meet Phil Ordway."

"The possibilities are about zero, and I am not interested in meeting this Phil Ordway," Garth said bluntly. At that moment Bev Middleton bustled in from the kitchen to clear the table. Ryan retreated into brooding silence.

"Well, now, how was everything?" the housekeeper demanded expectantly.

"Just as I'd remembered it, Bev," Devon assured her politely.

The only one at the table who seemed to pick up on the irony of her words was Garth. He gave Devon a narrow glance and then went to work on the huge slice of apple pie Bev had put in front of him.

Five

Devon awakened at dawn the next morning. Sounds of the already stirring household filtered into her consciousness. Garth Saxon rose early, and, therefore, so did everyone else around him. Devon yawned and made a sleepy grimace. The truth was, she was accustomed to getting up early herself. Old habits die hard. Apparently a year in the city hadn't been long enough to change them. Pushing back the heavy, faded quilt, she got out of bed and started toward the small bathroom that adjoined the bedroom.

En route she paused to examine the dreary beige curtains that were undoubtedly a legacy of the former owners along with almost everything else in the house. The curtains harmonized perfectly with the dreary beige carpet. The room was neat as a pin, naturally. Bev Middleton saw to that. But nothing compensated for the old, neglected feeling given off by the furnishings. The former owners had probably ordered everything out of a catalog

and thought they'd been terribly modern in their tastes.
They'd done the whole house in shades of beige and
brown.

Devon shuddered delicately and went on into the bathroom. Even when she'd been scraping by on a tight bud-
get while raising Lee and Kurt she'd managed to make her
home more interesting than this. If nothing else, she could
view the task of putting some life into Garth's home as a
challenge. She'd always had a flair for design. She could
do a lot with this place. The basic room proportions
weren't bad and with a wall knocked down here and there
and some windows added the house might take on some
real style. On that thought Devon stepped into the shower.

Half an hour later she arrived in the big kitchen downstairs to find Ryan and a couple of men in boots and den-
ims sitting around the old, oval table. Ryan was digging
into a pile of pancakes and the two men were helping
themselves to coffee. Bev was busy at the stove. There was
no sign of Garth.

Everyone glanced up and said good-morning as Devon
walked to the table. The two men eyed her with polite curiosity, introducing themselves casually as Steve and Cal.
They had been working for Garth for the past several
months, one of them explained. One of the perks of the
job, it seemed, consisted of several cups of Bev's coffee
while they discussed the day's work with the boss.

"You're up bright and early this morning," Bev observed as she threw bacon into the frying pan. "Thought
maybe you'd want to sleep in."

"How could I sleep in with the smell of your coffee filling the house?" Devon grinned and helped herself to the
pot. Bev Middleton might have limited notions of what
constituted dinner but she did make first-rate coffee.

Bev looked pleased. "Garth'll be in shortly. He ducked outside before breakfast to check on the progress the builder made yesterday on the new barn."

The tanned, lanky man who had called himself Cal chuckled. "Garth figures the whole place might fall apart if he's gone for more than eight hours."

Ryan raised his eyebrows. "I'll bet he packed you up in a hurry and hustled you back here right quick yesterday, huh, Devon?"

"Faster than a speeding bullet." Devon took a sip of the strong, hot coffee.

"That's my big brother. Always organizes things so that he gets what he wants. The rest of us aren't always so lucky." The bitterness in Ryan's voice was audible to everyone in the kitchen. Steve and Cal paid great attention to their coffee and Bev concentrated on frying bacon.

Only Devon offered Ryan a quietly sympathetic glance. "Is that the morning paper you've got there?" she asked, searching for a polite way to break the awkward silence.

Ryan nodded, handing it to her. "Sure. You want it?"

"Just the financial section." Devon reached across the table. "I took a flyer in the stock market a couple of months ago. Since then I've developed this obsessive interest in the financial sections of newspapers. Even the comic pages come second these days."

Ryan's expression brightened. "No kidding? What did you buy?"

"Just a couple of little penny stocks. One mining outfit in Colorado and a tiny software firm in Washington. A hundred shares each." Devon flipped through the paper to find the previous day's stock listings.

Ryan leaned forward intently. "While you're checking, take a look at a firm called Ethelton Green Creations. My broker talked me into a hundred shares last week."

"Over the counter?"

"Right."

Devon agreeably ran her finger down the over-the-counter listings. "Here we go. Ethelton Green. Six and a half."

"Hey, not bad." Ryan was already out of his chair. "I bought that sucker at four." He leaned over Devon's shoulder to verify her report. "Two and a half points in one week."

"Watch out or you'll get rich," Devon teased. "Now let me look at my little winners. Aha, here we go. The mining stock is down a point and the other one is up a point. Must be my lucky day. I'm actually breaking even."

Ryan grinned. "Unless you count brokerage commissions."

Steve and Cal stared at the other two in silence. It was obvious the stock market was a foreign world to them. Bev had nothing to contribute to the conversation either. When Garth strode into the kitchen from the back porch he found Devon and Ryan with their heads together intently discussing P/E ratios, short sales and options.

"What the devil's got you two so fascinated with the paper this morning?" he demanded dourly as he sat down next to Devon and reached for the coffee. He seemed to fill the warm, cozy room, dominating it with his presence. Steve and Cal greeted him with an easy informality, but there was no doubt about the quiet respect that underlined their words. The boss was back.

"Ryan and I were just checking our stocks," Devon explained. She smiled sunnily at Garth, ignoring the remote, forbidding quality that was emanating from him.

Garth was always sober looking and sober acting, but this morning he seemed downright grim. She wondered what was bothering him. "Ryan's making money and I'm breaking even. Not bad, huh?"

"You two are involved in the stock market?" He shot both offenders a hard glare. "Of all the damn fool ideas. What did you do? Let some fast-talking broker open an account and sell you a bunch of junk? Might as well go out and buy a lottery ticket." His gaze pinned Devon. "How much have you thrown away, Devon?"

She refolded the paper, taking her time in the process. Ryan quietly resumed his seat. "We're not married yet, Garth. My finances are still my own private business."

"The hell they are. If you've got no more sense than to get into the stock market, then you're damn well going to get some advice from me on your *private business*."

Devon grinned, aware that everyone else in the room was feeling extremely uncomfortable as they watched the small scene. "Advice, Garth? Have you got any hot tips?" she asked ingenuously.

"If you've got any extra cash to invest, you can put it into something solid, like land."

"Oh, I couldn't possibly afford California real estate. I'll stick to my little speculative stocks. At least they do something interesting every day. Land just sits there. Very boring."

"Of all the idiotic nonsense," Garth exploded tightly. He was about to add to that when he seemed to become aware at last of the fact that he had an audience. "We will discuss this later, Devon," he concluded grimly.

"Later might be too late," she pointed out. "I might have lost my shirt in the market by then."

"That's enough for now, Devon," Garth growled.

"On the other hand," Devon went on thoughtfully, "I might be rich."

"I said that's enough."

"Of course, I may get lucky with my lottery ticket this week and that will solve all my problems, won't it? Has anyone seen the winning numbers yet?"

"Devon."

When Garth used that tone everyone shut up. Devon was no exception, but she knew from the looks being exchanged by the others that as far as they were concerned, she had definitely won the small confrontation that had just taken place over the breakfast table.

It was Bev Middleton who made a gallant effort to defuse the situation. She set down a heaping platter of pancakes in front of Garth and another in front of Devon. "Now, then, have you two talked about the wedding arrangements? I'll want to do some shopping, you know. Didn't you say you were going to have the ceremony in the minister's office next Saturday morning, Garth?"

Devon opened her mouth before Garth could. "Oh, that's all been changed, Bev."

"Changed?" Bev looked honestly confused. People seldom changed plans made by Garth Saxon.

"That's right," Devon assured her. "I've decided we're going to make an occasion out of this. If you can't celebrate a wedding in style, what can you celebrate? The ceremony will take place at the end of the month. That will give you and me time to address invitations, Bev. We'll have the reception here, of course. A buffet, I think, with plenty of champagne. Better plan for about two hundred. We'll hire people to help clean up since Garth and I won't be able to stick around afterward. He and I will be leaving immediately after the reception."

Bev was looking dumbfounded. "Leaving?" she managed, sending a questioning glance toward Garth, who was giving his full attention to his pancakes. "For where?"

"Hawaii. We'll be gone a week," Devon informed her blithely.

Steve and Cal stared first at Devon and then at Garth.

"A whole week?" Steve asked blankly.

Garth didn't look up from his food. "You heard her."

Cal choked discreetly on his coffee. "I see."

It was Ryan who dared to voice the amazement of the others. "A week in Hawaii, big brother? Aren't you afraid Hawk's Flight will crumble into ruin while you're gone? And a reception for two hundred? We all know how you hate large parties. This is fascinating. Much more interesting than the stock market. A whole new world could be opening up here. Garth Saxon: gentleman socialite."

Garth finished his meal and got to his feet. "There's one thing Devon got wrong."

Devon held her breath but she kept her inquiring smile very serene. "What's that, Garth?"

"The wedding," he announced flatly, "will be in three weeks, not a month."

Her smile widened, but she merely nodded obediently. It was obviously nothing more than a desperate effort to reclaim some semblance of control over the matter, and she didn't begrudge it. The poor man was undoubtedly feeling backed into a corner. A dangerous situation for all concerned. She knew she would be wise to surrender a small battle in exchange for the larger victory. "Three weeks," she agreed.

He didn't appear particularly mollified, but at least he let the matter drop. Garth turned to face his half brother. "You look like you've had enough pancakes, Ryan. You can give Cal and me a hand down at the new barn. As long as you're going to hang around, you might as well earn your keep. Steve, you were supposed to be fixing the fence in the south pasture today, as I recall. Let's get moving, folks. The day is half over.''

He led the way out of the kitchen and the other men followed obediently. But Ryan, about to be the last male out the door, paused to throw Devon a cheerful grin and a wink. Then the screen door slammed behind him.

Bev watched the men leave and then plunked down at the table across from Devon. She poured herself a big cup of coffee, leaned her elbows on the table and gave Devon a long, considering look.

"Well, well, well," Bev Middleton murmured. "Going in for a bit of lion taming these days, eh?"

"You know as well as I do, Bev, that if this marriage is going to work, there will have to be a few changes made around here."

Bev nodded. "I always did say that if any woman could change Garth, it would be you. No one else stands a chance. I'm impressed. How in the world did you convince him to take a week-long honeymoon in Hawaii? That man hasn't been off this ranch for more than twenty-four hours since the day he bought it."

"He needs a vacation."

"True. It'll be good for him. Won't hurt him to have a big wedding and reception, either. He hasn't bothered to entertain his neighbors since he arrived in Hawk Springs. Oh, if someone drops by, he's generous enough. He'll invite 'em to stay for drinks and dinner. But he's never gone in for much socializing."

"He probably doesn't know how," Devon said thoughtfully. "He used to be married, you know. I imagine his ex-wife handled that side of things for him."

"The divorce was hard on him," Bev said. "He'd been free almost a year when he bought this place and moved here, but I could tell he was still affected by what had happened. He never talked much about his ex-wife, of course. Garth isn't the type to tell you about himself. No one in town knows much about his past other than the fact that he owns a fair amount of land here in California and some over in Arizona. He knows ranching inside out, he works hard and he's whip smart when it comes to business. That's about all anyone is ever likely to learn about him." Bev paused and then said in a low, meaningful tone, "She ran off with another man, you know."

"He mentioned it." Devon took a sip of coffee.

"Hard on a man's pride when something like that happens."

Devon shrugged. "Equally hard on a woman's pride when her husband runs off with another woman."

Bev smiled. "You're absolutely right, of course. And I guess it happens all the time these days, doesn't it?"

"All the time."

Bev poured more coffee. "That's one problem you won't ever have to worry about, though."

"Garth running off with another woman?" Devon shook her head, aware of a deep sense of certainty and satisfaction. "No, I won't, will I? Garth doesn't do things that way. He's up front and honest about everything. He'd never sneak around behind my back with another woman."

"He's a hard man, Devon, but he's a good man. He just needs a little softening up around the edges."

"I'm going to try, Bev," Devon told her with sudden resolution. "Let's just hope I don't get pulverized in the process."

"Are you kidding? That man has been putty in your hands since the day he met you."

Devon stared at her, astounded, and then she burst out laughing. "If Garth is an example of putty in my hands, I'd hate to be holding something hard."

Bev grinned a woman-to-woman sort of grin. "I expect Garth could arrange that, too, but knowing him, it won't happen in this house until he's got a ring on your finger. If you ask me, it's too bad he's so determined to wait."

Devon's brows rose. "I had no idea you had such racy notions, Bev."

"I think Garth would be a much happier man if he were sleeping with you now, instead of holding off until after the wedding. A man like him needs a woman. He's been too long without one."

Devon flushed, remembering Garth's lazy contentment after he had made love to her in her San Francisco flat. His mood had definitely changed for the better until she'd ruined everything by suggesting they have an affair instead of getting married. "I'll keep your advice in mind, Bev. Let's talk about something else."

"Such as?"

"Dinner. Take the evening off. I'm going to cook tonight."

Bev looked surprised and then she nodded. "Suits me. Might take in a movie with my sister. There's a new film down at the theater."

"What's it called?" When Bev told her, Devon chuckled. "It's good. I saw it several months ago in San Francisco. Figures it's just hitting Hawk Springs now." She got to her feet. "I'm going to go shopping for groceries later this morning. Which car shall I use?"

"I usually take the station wagon into town for groceries. The keys are by the front door. But I've got plenty of stuff in the freezer. No need to go the market."

"That's all right," Devon told her firmly. "I feel like something fresh for dinner."

In the end, she wound up going to the market in Ryan's shiny red sports car. He came back to the house about midmorning to pick up some tools and when he saw Devon about to leave in the station wagon, he obligingly tossed her the keys to his car.

"Here, no need to embarrass yourself on the road in that tank," he said easily. "Take mine. It'll look much better on you than that station wagon."

"Thanks, Ryan, I appreciate it. I'll be very careful. How are you and Garth doing today?"

Ryan grimaced. "Just fine as long as I don't bring up the subject of going into business with Phil Ordway." He hesitated in the doorway for a moment. "You know, I didn't think Garth would get you back here. I thought once you were free, you'd be smart enough to stay gone. Are you sure you know what you're doing, Devon?"

"No, but Garth is." She tossed the keys into the air and walked out the door. "See you later."

She spotted Garth in the rearview mirror as she pulled out of the drive in the shiny little car. He didn't look pleased with her choice of vehicle. She put her hand out the window and waved cheerily.

The new supermarket was a definite improvement over the small, old-fashioned grocery store where Devon had shopped when she lived in Hawk Springs. These aisles were a good deal less congested, but it still wasn't easy to make her way down them because everyone she saw wanted to stop and chat. Almost everyone recognized her and curiosity was rampant. Devon decided to be forthright and blasé about the entire subject of her return to town.

"Oh, yes, haven't you heard?" she found herself saying over and over again. "Garth and I are going to be married in three weeks. Yes, it's been quite a long engagement. You know Garth, he never does anything in a hurry. Likes to think about his decisions. You'll be getting an invitation to the wedding this week. Please plan on coming. We'd love to have you."

She had repeated the litany a dozen times before she rounded the bread counter and nearly collided with an attractive young woman her own age.

"Excuse me," Devon said quickly, narrowly averting a collision of shopping carts.

"My fault. I shouldn't have been standing in the middle of the aisle." The woman regarded her with deep interest. "I'm Rita Dennison. I couldn't help overhearing what you were saying to Mrs. Bridger. You're marrying Garth Saxon?" Rita had a sunny smile, a ponytail and a pair of inquiring brown eyes. She was dressed in a pair of jeans and a T-shirt.

"That's right," Devon said easily. She reached down for a package of rice. "The only Dennison I knew when I left town last year was one named Sam. He had a ranch not far from Garth's stud farm. Any connection?"

"I married Sam a few months ago. I used to live in San Diego."

"Quite a switch."

"I grew up on a farm, but I never thought I'd marry a country boy. When I went to college I had a lawyer or a business executive in mind." Rita laughed. "But things change."

"I know the feeling. I had a few plans myself when I left town a year ago." Devon had the distinct impression she was going to like Rita Dennison.

The conversation in the aisle went on for another fifteen minutes before Rita said impulsively, "Listen, Sam and I are having a big barbecue on Sunday to celebrate finishing our new house. We invited Garth last week, but he said he couldn't make it. Said he already had plans for this weekend. Any chance you could change his mind?"

Devon smiled slowly. "As it happens, I know for a fact that Garth's plans for this weekend have changed drastically. We'll be glad to come to your barbecue."

"Great. Bring anyone else you'd like along. It's going to be my first major party and I'm terrified that no one will show."

Devon thought of Ryan. "Okay, I'll see if I can drum up some business. We'll see you Sunday afternoon, Rita."

"I'm delighted. I'm glad to find someone else my own age living nearby."

Devon laughed and started down the aisle with a pleased feeling. She wondered what Garth would say when she told him she'd accepted an invitation on his behalf.

As it turned out Garth was more alarmed by the absence of Bev Middleton that evening than he was by the information that Devon had planned to attend the party. He paced into the kitchen after washing up for dinner and glared at Devon.

"Where's Bev?"

"Having dinner with her sister. Afterward they're both going to a movie. Go on into the living room, Garth, we're going to have some wine before dinner."

Ryan appeared in the doorway. "Now that sounds like an absolutely brilliant suggestion. I'll pour."

Garth ignored the byplay. "Bev is supposed to be here every night."

"She'll be back in plenty of time to save your reputation, Garth," Devon assured him. "Calm down and go into the living room. I'll be in as soon as I put the rice on to cook."

"Damn it, it's not my reputation I'm worried about, Devon. I don't want people talking about you."

He was interrupted by Ryan, who was inhaling with great pleasure. "Smells good," Ryan observed, examining the label on the bottle of white wine he'd found in the refrigerator. "What's for dinner?"

"Chicken curry with all the condiments. I actually found a bottle of chutney in the new supermarket."

"Ah, civilization strikes Hawk Springs at last." Ryan deftly removed the cork from the bottle and picked up three glasses. "Garth, you've never had it so good. Let's go work up an appetite in the appropriate manner."

Garth cast an odd look at Devon but finally turned to follow his brother into the living room. Devon went after them as soon as she'd turned down the heat on the rice. She found both men waiting for her, their glasses filled. She sank down onto the old sofa and lifted her glass.

Casually she told Garth and Ryan about the invitation to the Dennisons'. Garth thought about it, shrugged and finally nodded. He sipped his wine as Devon went on to tell Ryan he was invited also.

"If I'm still here, I'll go with you," Ryan agreed. "My plans aren't settled yet." He glanced at Garth who ignored him.

For a moment Devon was afraid Ryan might ruin the beginning of the evening by bringing up the subject of his business plans, but he refrained. Gratefully she guided the conversation into less threatening channels. Garth needed this little evening ritual to unwind after a hard day's work, she told herself. She wanted to avoid controversial topics.

By the time dinner was served Garth was looking more relaxed than he had all day. He sat down to the chicken curry with a dubious expression, but it wasn't long before he was asking for seconds.

The evening passed without incident. Ryan read the evening paper and watched television while Garth clobbered Devon three times in a row over a checkerboard. Apparently vastly satisfied with his victories, he then announced he was going to do some work in his study. He disappeared, leaving Ryan and Devon behind in the living room.

Ryan was silent for a moment before observing, "This is the best mood he's been in for months. I'd better strike while the iron is hot." He got to his feet.

Devon winced. "Maybe you should wait a couple of days, Ryan."

"I can't. I haven't got the time. Phil wants to move now and I have to know if I'm going to get Garth's backing."

"I don't think his mood has changed enough to make him want to give you money, Ryan," Devon warned.

"All I'm going to try for tonight is to get Garth to agree to at least talk to Phil."

"Good luck."

"Thanks, I'll need it."

Devon picked up a magazine without glancing at the title. She turned the pages absently while she listened for sounds of an explosion from the study.

There was silence for a reassuring length of time and as she grew less tense, Devon took more notice of what she was reading. It was, predictably enough, a magazine for breeders and buyers of Arabian horses and it was more than a year old. She was about to toss it back down onto the stack when she saw a familiar photograph of Royal Standard. The stallion was posed in all his arrogant beauty, his small delicate ears at attention, fine nostrils flared and smoothly muscled shoulders well displayed. The equine intelligence and quivering vitality of the animal came through brilliantly.

Devon had worked for hours getting Royal Standard so beautifully posed. Garth had handled the stallion while she took her shots. The result had been pretty good, even if she did say so herself.

The page with the photograph had been well thumbed, Devon noted. She realized that Garth must have turned to it many times. She was thinking about Garth sitting alone here in the evenings studying the photo she'd taken of the stallion, when the long-delayed explosion finally occurred in the study.

Actually, it was Ryan's voice she heard most clearly. He was arguing passionately while Garth, as usual, was under full control. Garth never yelled. He didn't have to raise his voice to accomplish his goals. Ultimately he was always in charge and he knew it. So did everyone else around him. The outcome was quite predictable. Ryan eventually gave up and stormed out of the study. He headed straight upstairs, without bothering to say good-night to Devon. The study door slammed behind him and remained ominously closed.

Devon waited five long minutes and then she got up, went into the kitchen and took down the ancient brandy bottle from the high cupboard where it was stored between Christmas and Thanksgiving. Bottle in hand, she went down the hall to the study and knocked.

Without waiting for an answer she opened the door and stepped inside. Garth was sitting behind his desk, his face a grim mask as he examined some account books open in front of him. He looked up with a forbidding expression as the door opened and then he relaxed slightly.

"I thought you might need this," Devon said, tipping the brandy bottle over a small glass and handing the drink to him.

"Ryan's the one who needs the drink, but I'll take it. That boy is going to succeed in making me lose my temper one of these days."

"I think," Devon said gently as she sat down on the other side of the desk, "you're going to have to stop thinking of him as a boy."

"How can I do that as long as he's coming up with these hare-brained schemes?" Garth took a long swallow of the brandy.

"Can't you give him a chance with this particular scheme, Garth?"

He eyed her consideringly. "A chance? Have you any idea of how much money he's asking for?"

"No. And I didn't mean for you to just hand over the money. But you could agree to meet his partner."

"This so-called partner of his sounds fishy, Devon."

She sighed. "I'll admit you're usually right when it comes to judging people, but you haven't even met this guy."

"There's no need. I can tell from what Ryan says that this Phil Ordway is nothing but a fast-talking con man who's got his hooks into my brother. Probably thinks he can use Ryan to drain money out of Ryan's dumb rancher of a brother."

Devon smiled slightly. "Let Phil meet you and find out for himself that conning you out of a bundle of cash is going to be harder than taking the stripes off a tiger. A meeting between you and Ordway should settle things one way or another. And Ryan will know that at least you gave his plans some legitimate consideration.''

Garth watched her silently over the top of his brandy. ''His scheme doesn't deserve any legitimate consideration.''

''Maybe not, but Ryan does. He needs to know you have some respect for his judgment.''

Garth exhaled deeply. ''He isn't as easy to handle as Lee was. Hell, it's easier to handle my men than it is to handle my brother.''

''That's because he *is* your brother, Garth. I've told you that. It's always different when it's family. You've spent so long looking after him that it's hard for you to realize he can look after himself. Believe me, after raising Lee and Kurt, I know what I'm talking about.''

Garth took another sip of brandy and sat in silence for a long time. ''All right,'' he said finally. ''I'll tell Ryan he can invite Ordway here for a meeting. But no promises and definitely no financial commitments.''

Devon's smile grew gentle. ''Thanks, Garth. I think it will be an excellent way of handling the situation. Afterward you can still tell Ryan you're not interested in the deal. At least he'll know you've given it a chance. Just treat him as the intelligent person he is. Maybe he is way off base trying to go into business with Ordway, but a lot of more experienced people have made similar mistakes. It doesn't mean he's really lacking in judgment or common sense. He's just ambitious and anxious to make his mark in the world.''

''Mmm.'' Garth didn't look convinced but his gaze was a good deal less forbidding. ''Speaking of judgment and common sense, I've been intending to go over this nonsense of your being in the stock market.''

Devon took the last swallow from her glass and smiled sweetly. "I think you've got enough on your mind for now. Don't fret yourself about my little forays into the stock market. We can discuss it at another time."

His eyes gleamed with a mixture of amusement and masculine wariness. "Why do I get the feeling you've got a natural talent for leading me in the direction you want me to go?" He got slowly to his feet and came around the edge of the desk. "Maybe you're right. Maybe we should skip my lecture on the evils of the stock market tonight. God knows I've got a few other things besides that on my mind at the moment."

She looked up at him from beneath her lashes. "Such as?"

He reached down and hauled her lightly to her feet. "Such as wishing to hell you hadn't put the wedding off for three long weeks. The waiting may kill me."

His mouth captured hers with a sudden intensity that took away Devon's breath and called forth an immediate, vital response from her senses. Without any hesitation she put her arms around his neck and let herself melt against Garth's hard frame.

"Devon, honey, I want you so much. You don't know how it is for me. I spent last night lying awake for hours thinking about the night we spent in your apartment. I thought once I had you under my roof, the sleepless nights would be over. I should have known better." His lips roved over her cheek to the soft, scented place behind her ear and then he pushed her hair away from the back of her neck and kissed her on her nape.

Devon shivered and tightened her hold on him. He slid his hands down to her hips, lifting her, pulling her against the straining heat of his thighs. She could feel the taut, waiting need in him and it sent a thrill of love and excitement through her veins.

"Garth?"

"I know, babe, I know. Me, too." He leaned back against the desk and spread his booted feet wide. Then he urged her close, his big hands cupping her hips and anchoring her firmly between his jeaned legs. "Every time I think of my bed upstairs, just waiting for you, I want to haul you across the state line into Nevada and skip this whole wedding scene bit."

"Maybe you're being too hard on yourself. On both of us." She kissed the strong column of his neck. "Why should we wait? Ryan's gone to bed. Bev's not here. This is your house, Garth. You can do as you like."

He shuddered and caught her face between his hands, kissing her breathless. "You're right. Why the hell am I waiting? No one will know and I need you so much tonight...."

The sound of tires crunching gravel in the drive broke into the strained, sensual atmosphere of the small room, cutting off Garth's words before he could finish.

"Oh, hell," he said through set teeth. "That's Bev." Very carefully he put Devon away from him. "Go."

"Where?"

"Upstairs. To bed. Now. Move, woman."

Devon saw the flaring hunger in his eyes and smiled gently, teasingly. "Yes, sir, boss. I'm on my way. But if you're in another bad mood in the morning, don't blame me."

"I'll blame whoever I like for my bad moods," he informed her grimly. "Now disappear."

Devon disappeared. On her way up the stairs she thought a lot about old-fashioned males who went out of their way to protect their women from gossip.

Men like Garth Saxon were rare in today's world.

Six

Garth's familiar dour morning mood was worse than usual the next day when he showed up for breakfast. The strict, no-nonsense quality that seemed so characteristic of him was stronger than ever as he gave orders for the day's work. Steve and Cal drank coffee in silence and listened to the instructions without offering any comment. Ryan sat in stony sullenness on one side of the table. Devon tried a few casual remarks about the weather but Bev was the only one who responded. Even Bev, herself, seemed to be walking on eggs around Garth, along with everyone else.

Nothing lightened in the room until Garth finished his coffee and got to his feet. Halfway to the door, he turned to his half brother.

"You can invite this Phil Ordway to come here for a day. I'll sit down with the two of you and listen to your plans. But no guarantees. Clear?"

Ryan's sullenness vanished to be replaced by a relieved, thankful grin. "Perfectly clear, big brother. Thanks. I'll call him this morning. You won't regret this, I promise."

Garth's gaze went briefly to Devon's face. His mouth curved sardonically. "Let's hope not." The screen door slammed shut behind him and Steve and Cal.

There was a moment of silence in the cozy kitchen while Bev and Ryan stared at Devon, who calmly munched toast.

"I assume Garth's change of mind is your doing?" Ryan demanded cheerfully.

"Well, I did discuss the matter with him last night after you'd gone to bed," Devon admitted.

Bev chuckled, nodding in satisfaction. "It was her doing, all right. Not much on the face of this earth that can change Garth's mind once he's made a decision."

"Except Devon?" Ryan offered.

"Except Devon," Bev agreed.

"Uh," said Devon cautiously, "I wouldn't get too carried away with the idea that I've got some magic power over him, if I were you. The simple truth is that I gave him a reasonable suggestion that, Garth, being a reasonable man, accepted."

Ryan's grin broadened. "Once Garth's mind is made up, he's no more susceptible to sweet reason than he is to any other force. No, Devon, it must have been magic. That's the only explanation."

"Woman magic," Bev elaborated. "Powerful stuff. Now, if you could just do something about his morning moods, we'd all get down on our knees and kiss your toes, Devon. That man hasn't exactly been a ray of sunshine in the mornings for the past year, but it seems to me that lately he's deteriorating."

"Yeah," Ryan observed. "He *is* getting worse, isn't he?"

Devon set her coffee cup down with a clatter. "If you two are finished chortling, I think I will excuse myself. There are some things I want to do today."

"Like what?" Bev asked curiously.

"I'm going to start with the living room. My furniture should be here soon and I have plans for it. This whole house needs a face-lift."

"But Garth just had it painted a couple months ago. I expect he was getting it ready for you."

"That was thoughtful of him," Devon said, "but this place needs a lot more than a paint job. Oh, and by the way, Bev, if you want to make plans for this evening again, feel free. I'll be handling the evening meals from now on. You've got your hands full as it is."

Bev looked surprised, but not displeased. "All the evening meals?"

"If you don't mind."

"Heck, no, I don't mind. Back when the Simpsons had this place, I just took care of lunch for the Simpsons and their hands and did the housecleaning. Mrs. Simpson handled breakfast and dinner. I only started in full-time when Garth bought Hawk's Flight and needed someone to look after him."

"The arrangements you had with the Simpsons will work out fine after Garth and I are married," Devon decided.

"Sounds good to me," Bev announced.

Ryan glanced at his watch. "I can't wait to call Phil. He'll be in his office in a couple of hours. What a break. This is going to make all the difference in the world." He surged to his feet and gave Devon a quick, brotherly hug. "Thanks, Devon. I really appreciate this."

"I hope it works out," she said wryly," but frankly, I wouldn't count on anything, if I were you. Garth can be awfully stubborn."

"He wouldn't have told me to invite Phil here unless he was willing to at least listen seriously to our plans," Ryan assured her. Whistling, he strode out of the kitchen.

Bev smiled knowingly at Devon. "As soon as word gets out you can wrap Garth around your little finger, you're going to have all sorts of folks coming to you asking you to speak to Garth for them."

Devon shook her head mournfully. "I don't know why everyone thinks I'm wrapping him around my little finger. All I did was speak to the man."

The phone rang before Bev could respond to that. Devon was closest and automatically she reached out to pick up the receiver. The caller asked for Mr. Saxon, and when Devon told him he wasn't immediately available, the voice on the other end of the line explained his business.

Devon listened politely, told the man who she was and then proceeded to handle the matter at hand. By the time she got off the phone, Bev was staring at her.

"That was McShaney?" Bev asked bluntly. "The McShaney who's been talking about buying one of Garth's colts?"

"The same, I gather." Devon was busily jotting down notes to herself on a pad.

"You invited him and his wife to stay here overnight when they come to see the colts?" Bev was looking distinctly disconcerted.

"Of course. Can't expect them to stay at the motel on the other side of town. You know as well as I do, that place is a dump. They'll be much more comfortable here. We've got plenty of bedrooms. They won't be arriving until next month and by then I'll have this place looking like it belongs in the current decade instead of the 1950s.''

"Yes, but that's not the point. Garth's never done business that way. He invites people here to see the horses, but he doesn't entertain them, if you know what I mean.''

"This is big business, Bev. Have you any idea how much money is involved in the sale of just one of Garth's prize colts? We're talking thousands of dollars. With that kind of money at stake, a businessman should expect to entertain a client occasionally.''

Bev gave her a speculative glance. "It'll be interesting to see what Garth says when he finds out.''

"Yes it will, won't it?'' Devon agreed with an airy attitude that belied her inner uncertainty. She went outside into the rapidly warming morning to find the master of the house.

He was exactly where she had expected to find him, peering over the shoulder of the contractor who was building the new barn. When she hailed him, he frowned in her direction, said something to the builder and then strode over to where Devon was standing.

"What's up?'' he asked briskly.

She told him about the impending visit from the buyer and Garth listened attentively until she got to the part about inviting McShaney and his wife to stay the night.

"You did what?''

"I invited them to stay here, Garth. They'll be spending the whole day talking business with you. You can't send them down the road to that rundown motel on the other side of Hawk Springs. That place will make a very bad impression.''

"I'm not out to make a good impression on McShaney. I'm trying to sell him a horse!''

"You're a businessman, Garth. You have to act like one."

"This may come as a shock to you, Devon, but I've been doing just fine taking care of business in my own way."

She smiled brilliantly. "You'll do even better when you try it my way. Trust me, Garth. I know what I'm doing. I've spent a year in the big city, remember? For twelve months I've been working for successful businesses of all kinds. I've learned a lot. When you're involved in the kind of money these horses bring, it's important to be gracious and hospitable. Creates a good image."

"But I don't have the time to entertain buyers!" he exploded.

Devon's smile didn't alter. "You've got me to handle that side of things for you. You wanted to marry a woman who would be a working partner here at Hawk's Flight. Okay, you've got a working partner. Me."

He gave her a curious, burning look. "Is that right?"

"That's right, Garth."

Devon felt him testing her willpower in some silent, intense fashion she didn't quite understand. She wondered what it was he wanted to discover. But nothing was said and after a moment Garth simply nodded brusquely. "All right, we'll give it a try your way. I've been trying to close this deal with McShaney for four months. If it settles next month, I'll admit you might know what you're doing."

"And if it doesn't settle next month?"

"Then," he said smoothly, "you'll admit that doing things your way is a waste of time and effort and we'll go back to doing them my way." He started to turn and then paused. "Why don't you get your camera out this afternoon? It's time we updated the ads for Royal Standard and High Flyer. You could take some preliminary shots. Get some ideas together. I'd like to do something that'll really get attention this time.''

Devon nodded agreeably. She leaned against a fence, gazing out toward a small cluster of mares grazing in the pasture. "Have you thought about putting together a brochure for Hawk's Flight, Garth? You know, one of those slick, glossy things that can be mailed to prospective buyers or people who are in the market for stud service. Something classy and upscale."

He shrugged. "I know what you mean. I've seen promotional pamphlets from other stud farms. It would be a lot of work."

"I did some photography and layout work this past year and I had some experience with it in college. With the help of a good printer, I could handle the job."

He smiled faintly. "When I thought of you as a partner here I had visions of you planting a garden and supervising the house."

"You didn't see me getting involved in the business end of things?" she asked with a teasing light in her eyes.

He took a deep breath and let it out in a long, considering sigh as he leaned against the fence beside her. "Truth is, I don't think I thought much beyond getting you here and keeping you here on a permanent basis. I guess I didn't sit down and make a list of things I thought you'd handle. I knew you'd be busy. Seems like there's always plenty to do around a place this size."

True enough, Devon thought in amusement. Any rancher's or farmer's wife could testify to that fact. Her own mother had always worked as hard as her father, and Devon knew every successful farm and ranch in the vicinity had a woman on it who was as involved in the day-to-day business as her husband. It had been that way for families that worked the land and raised animals since time immemorial.

The knowledge of just how much work was involved and how long the hours could be on a ranch or a farm was what drove many young women to the city to look for a different way of life.

But there was a certain unique satisfaction to the lifestyle, too, Devon told herself as she gazed out over the green fields and sleek Arabians. For the first time, she could admit to herself that she hadn't really found everything she'd wanted in the city. A part of her had missed the land and the feeling of dealing in the basics of life.

"I'll dig out my camera after lunch," she said softly. "Taking pictures of horses will be a change from the kind of free-lance photography I did in San Francisco."

"What kind of photography was that?" Garth asked curiously.

"Well, on one job I got to take pictures of screwdrivers and drills for a manufacturer's catalog. You have no idea how hard it is to make screwdrivers and electric drills look colorful and interesting. On another assignment I spent a couple of weeks shooting furnaces and heat pumps."

"Sounds dull."

"It was." Devon laughed softly. "When I got really fed up I went to Golden Gate Park and took pictures of tourists taking pictures of squirrels. To tell you the truth, those were my best shots."

"You were meant to work with living creatures, Devon, not mechanical, city things. You belong here in the country."

Devon couldn't think of anything to say to that so she said good-morning and returned to the house. There was plenty to do, including planning a wedding.

* * *

The remainder of the week passed quickly. Ryan announced Phil Ordway would be arriving on Sunday and he intended to take him to the party at the Dennisons' that evening. Ryan was elated with his plans to introduce Phil and Garth.

Garth's morning moods didn't lighten and there were days when Devon wondered just how much he'd slept during the night. There was a taut, drawn expression around his eyes that told its own tale some mornings and he went through a lot of coffee before he left the house.

Bev Middleton raised her brows in a knowing fashion a time or two after Garth lost his temper over some small matter, and Devon knew the older woman assumed everything would change when Garth had a woman in his bed.

Devon wasn't so sure, but she found herself plowing ahead with the wedding plans. She was committed now and every day seemed to reinforce the sense of commitment. It was as if having been forced to face Hawk Springs again, she was somehow free to confront her love for Garth. It flowered daily, driving out a year's worth of doubts and fear.

Her precious furniture arrived on Friday and Devon took advantage of Garth's absence from the stud farm to have the movers install the pieces exactly where she wanted them. She had given the matter a great deal of thought and was generally pleased with the outcome.

The living room needed a lot more work, but the addition of the black chairs and love seat, together with the odd pieces of rich red, did wonders for the old-fashioned room. Devon blithely commandeered Steve, Cal and Ryan to move the old brown-and-beige sofa and two massive chairs upstairs to one of the bedrooms.

When the deed was done everyone stood around, shaking their heads.

"Going to be interesting to see what Garth says," Bev finally declared.

"Looks great, Devon. Can't believe it's the same room," Ryan said. "Amazing what some new furniture can do for a place."

Cal looked dubious. "Sure is funny-lookin' furniture."

Steve sat down in one of the chairs. "Not too bad. You'd think it would be kind of uncomfortable from the looks of it, but it's not half-bad."

"The Italians are excellent furniture designers," Devon informed one and all. She was about to continue on the subject when she heard the pickup pull into the drive. Garth was home.

Everyone looked at everyone else.

"Got to go see about fixin' that gate," Steve announced and vanished.

"Guess I'll check on my pie," Bev said and disappeared.

"Garth wanted me to get that hay moved this afternoon," Cal remarked before melting out of sight.

Devon was left glaring at Ryan. "Well? Are you going to find something else to do, too?"

Ryan grinned. "You kidding? This, I want to see." He leaned back against the wall as Garth walked into the front room with his long, easy stride. Devon greeted him cheerfully and decided to take the bull by the horns.

"Guess what arrived today, Garth."

Garth started to respond to the question and then he saw what had happened to the room. His reaction was immediate and unambivalent.

"What the hell is this stuff doing in here?" he growled, shoving his hat back on his head and planting his big fists on his hips.

"I told you I had plans for it." Devon kept her tone calm and placid, but inside she was suddenly very nervous. She had never tested Garth's indulgence toward her quite this far. "Looks great, don't you think? Does wonders for this room."

"What happened to the couch?"

"It's upstairs in one of the bedrooms."

"So help me, Devon, I told you I didn't want this stuff in the living room. I was going to have it put into storage."

"I canceled the orders and had the movers put it in here, instead," she informed him equably. This wasn't going at all well, she realized. Perhaps she'd overstepped her bounds. This was still Garth's house, after all. She wasn't his wife yet. It was difficult to gauge just how angry he really was. Garth's mood had been very volatile all week.

"Devon, when I give an order around here, I expect it to be obeyed." He swung toward Ryan. "What do you think you're doing?"

Ryan held up a placating hand. "Just standing here, honest."

"Well, go stand somewhere else, damn it!"

"I'm gone," Ryan said and did a quick disappearing act through the door.

Garth turned back to Devon. His gaze held a wealth of seething intent. The master of Hawk's Flight was going to lay down the law. "All right, let's get this ironed out here and now. I told you I didn't want this silly furniture in the living room, didn't I?"

Devon lifted her chin. "Yes, you did, but I told you I did want it here. And if you'll just calm down and take a look, you'll have to admit it's terrific in here. Just what the place needed. This is going to be my living room, too, Garth, and I have a right to have some say in how it looks. You're reacting unreasonably. You're just mad because I didn't follow orders, not because you really think the furniture looks terrible.''

"You're right. How the damned furniture looks isn't as important as the fact that I told you I didn't want it in here.''

Devon gathered her internal resources. "Garth, I hate to break this to you, but in a marriage, you do not get to have everything your own way. Having a wife is not like owning a mare. I know you're accustomed to being the boss. I realize you're used to having everything done just as you want it. There's something about you that makes everyone around you cave in and give way to you. You've gotten spoiled. But things are going to change around here.

"You've told me you want a working marriage. A partnership. Well, *partner*, that means we both get to have our own way from time to time. And when it comes to this furniture, I'm going to have the final say. I know a great deal more about design and color than you do. I took a lot of classes in fine arts in college, remember? I say the furniture looks good in here and it's going to stay.''

Garth stared at her in mingled astonishment and outrage. "I don't believe this. You're going to go to the mat with me over a few pieces of furniture?'' He waved a hand at the dashing furniture in question. "You consider this junk worth a full-scale showdown between us?''

"No, but you apparently do. Look how hard you're fighting over a couple of chairs and a sofa.''

"It's the principle of the thing!'' he snapped.

"Exactly.''

They stood glaring at each other in taut silence for a long moment. Devon sensed just how unstable the situation was and wondered if she should give up and give in: But the line had to be drawn somewhere, she told herself. Garth had to learn that he wasn't getting a household convenience, he was getting a wife.

"I don't want this stuff in here, Devon."

"Why not? Why are you so opposed to it?" she demanded.

"Because it reminds me of the year you spent in San Francisco!"

That took her aback. Devon blinked uncertainly and then took a steadying breath. "I'm here now, Garth. And so is the furniture. The year in San Francisco is over. Neither me or my furniture is going back."

The clash of wills caused almost visible energy to arc in the room. And then, to Devon's overwhelming relief, it was Garth who finally ended the stare-down. He stalked past Devon, heading toward the door. Fingers wrapped around the doorknob, he stopped and slanted her a narrow-eyed glance.

"Sometimes I forget," he muttered, "just how stubborn you can be."

Devon tried a tentative smile. "That's funny. I never forget how stubborn you can be."

He said something unprintable under his breath and yanked the brim of his hat down low over his eyes. In that moment he reminded Devon of a hard-edged gunslinger from another century sizing up an opponent before deciding whether to accept a challenge. There was a cool, speculative gleam in his gaze as he surveyed her slender, determined figure.

"You *and* the furniture are both here to stay?"

Devon nodded once, not quite daring to say anything. Something vitally important had just been said between the two of them. And Garth seemed to recognize it, too.

He exhaled slowly, as if coming to a decision. "All right. If you give me your word I won't have to put up with any more talk about how you should have stayed in the city instead of coming back here to Hawk Springs with me, I'll let you keep the damned furniture." He opened the door and stepped out onto the porch. Then he paused again and looked back at her. "But don't get the idea you can manipulate me this easily every time you want something."

"No, Garth. And you have my word."

"And in the future, you will talk to me before you decide to override my orders."

"Yes, Garth."

He eyed her skeptically and then stepped back inside the house, closed the door behind him and came across the room to tower over her. "I was right. You're going to drive me crazy until I get that ring on your finger."

Her eyes widened, half in challenge and half in relieved amusement. She wasn't quite sure why she was relieved. Garth still looked very intimidating. Standing in front of her in his dusty boots, jeans and denim shirt, with the Stetson pulled low over his eyes, he was every inch the complete macho cowboy. "Do you think things will be a lot different between us once we're married?"

"I think," he told her forcefully, pulling her into his arms, "that things will be a lot different when we can finish our arguments in bed." His mouth came down on hers in a short, hard kiss that held the essence of his pent-up desire and the remnants of his outrage over the matter of the furniture.

As usual, Devon felt herself relaxing against him, her mouth opening under his in undisguised surrender. Garth

cut the kiss off almost as soon as he felt her answering response. When he lifted his head, his eyes were gleaming.

"Yeah," he muttered. "Things will be different. At least
I won't be wandering around with this never-ending ache
in my guts." He released her and headed toward the door
again. "See you at dinner."

"Yes, Garth."

"What are we having tonight?"

"Pasta primavera."

"Sounds Italian," he grumbled.

"I thought it would be appropriate under the circumstances." Devon smiled to herself as the door closed behind him with grand finality. Until this past week Garth
had never exhibited any particular curiosity about dinner.
Probably because he'd always known what to expect from
Bev Middleton's cooking.

Things were different these days.

Phil Ordway arrived on Sunday morning and Devon had
to admit, the man had style. He pulled up in a black
Porsche and emerged from the car's cockpit wearing the
latest in trendy menswear: a slouchy, unconstructed linen
jacket, jeans that had never been near a ranch until now
and a pair of boots that would have been the pride of any
Texas oil baron.

Ordway was a good-looking man in his early thirties
who had the confidence, polish and style to make most
people think he would go far. He gave the impression he
intended to take Ryan with him. Ryan greeted him eagerly
and made introductions with an expansive air.

"You're not quite what I expected, Devon," Phil told
her with an engaging smile as he examined her stylish hair
and the sophisticated pleated pants and knit top she was

wearing. "Ryan told me folks out here tended to be real 'country.'"

"We have our moments," she told him dryly.

"Devon's an exception to the rule," Ryan said with a laugh. "She's just moved back here from San Francisco. She's bringing a little sophistication into Garth's mundane life."

"I see." Ordway smiled at Devon with easy charm.

"I understand you'll be staying the night?" Devon asked politely.

"If that's all right with you. I hate to impose, but I imagine it's going to take most of the afternoon to put our proposal to Mr. Saxon, and frankly, it's a hell of a long drive to the nearest decent-size town."

"It's no trouble. I'm sure Ryan told you we have a social engagement tonight, but you're welcome to join us."

"The barbecue sounds amusing. Haven't been to one in years." Phil glanced toward the barns. "Ah, is that your brother, Ryan?"

Ryan squared his shoulders. "That's him. Don't let him intimidate you, Phil."

Phil smiled enigmatically, his eyes cool and slightly amused. "Oh, I doubt he'll do that. I'm sure he just needs to have the details of our proposal spelled out for him in simple English. After all, he can't have had much experience with this kind of business. What would a man who's lived all his life on a ranch know about the ins and outs of creative financing?"

Ryan glanced uneasily at his friend as Devon cleared her throat and said, "Uh, Phil, I don't think you should assume Garth's not much of a businessman. The fact is, he's very shrewd."

Phil's smile widened. "I'm sure I can educate him. We'll keep things nice and simple and not bother him with a lot of detail."

Devon took one look at the remote, assessing expression on Garth's face as he approached, and suddenly she felt a little sorry for Phil Ordway and Ryan. "Lots of luck," she murmured to Ryan. It was too late to offer any other advice or sympathy. Garth was on them.

The three men spent the afternoon closeted in Garth's study. As the time wore on, Devon began glancing anxiously at the clock. They were all due at the Dennisons' by six and she didn't want to be late. She knew Rita Dennison would be nervous until people started showing up. But this meeting was very important to Ryan and she didn't dare interrupt it.

"What do you think is happening in that study, Bev?" Devon asked as she shared a pot of tea with the housekeeper around four-thirty.

"I expect Mr. Ordway is learning that Garth isn't exactly stupid when it comes to handing out money."

Devon's mouth curved. "I'm afraid you're right. I only hope Ordway has enough sense not to treat Garth as though he were a backwoods hick who's never seen a balance sheet. This meeting is so important to Ryan."

"Stop worrying about it, Devon," Bev advised in a motherly fashion. "You set it up and gave Ryan the chance. Now he has to handle the rest of it himself."

"I know." Devon drained her tea. "I think I'll go take my shower and get dressed. At least one of us will be ready to leave for the Dennisons' on time."

She dawdled through a leisurely shower and then spent quite a while choosing her outfit for the evening. This was to be the first time she had appeared in public as Garth's fiancée and she wanted to make an impression. After much consideration, she finally chose a graceful casual skirt in a vivid paisley print and paired it with a laced, tunic-style top. She experimented with the lacing for several minutes until she was satisfied she'd achieved the right look.

When she was finished, she opened her bedroom door and found Garth standing on the other side, his hand raised to knock.

"I was just checking to see if you're ready," he said, his eyes moving swiftly over her clothes. He was wearing a Western-cut jacket, an open-neck white shirt and a pair of close-fitting slacks. His hair was still damp from the shower.

"Ready and waiting. How did the meeting with Ordway go?"

"The guy's a jerk."

"Oh, poor Ryan."

"Poor Ryan's going to have to learn to tell the difference between con artists and real businessmen." Garth was frowning at the artfully unlaced tunic. "Aren't you going to finish tying that thing?"

"No, it's supposed to be left sort of half-unlaced."

"The hell it is. Lean over the way it is now and anyone standing in front of you is going to have a clear shot all the way to your...never mind. Just finish tying it and let's get going. It's getting late."

"But, Garth..." She started to protest and then sighed, remembering the battle over the furniture. She'd had the chief victory of the week, she could afford to be gracious now. Without another word she finished tying the laces of the tunic. When Garth took her hand and started downstairs, she asked, "Is Phil still going to be staying the night?"

"I guess so. I left him and Ryan in the study. I don't think Ordway's quite given up yet, but personally I've had enough 'creative financing' for one afternoon."

"Well, even if it didn't work out, I'm glad you gave Ryan a chance. Thank you, Garth." Impulsively, she stood on her toes to brush a soft kiss across his mouth.

He looked down at her as she pulled away, his gaze full of a waiting heat. Deliberately he drew one fingertip across her lower lip with a deep sensuality that made Devon shiver with expectation. "You're not angry because I didn't let myself get talked into financing Ryan's project?"

"Of course not. I only wanted you to give it fair consideration. You said you would and I'm sure you did. That's all anyone can ask."

His mouth kicked up at the corner. "You've got a lot of faith in my integrity."

"Not a lot of faith, Garth. *Complete* faith. You can be stubborn as a mule at times, but I'd trust your integrity to hell and back," Devon said simply.

His gray eyes darkened with sudden intensity. "It works both ways, you know," he said softly. "After the disaster of my last marriage I decided my main requirement in a wife was a sense of honor. I wanted a woman I could trust. I trust you, Devon."

"I'm glad," she whispered, wondering how close trust was to love.

He moved his rough fingertip across her lower lip again. "Soon, honey. Very soon. Have I told you, Devon Ellwood, that I'm never going to let you go?"

"No, but I think I was beginning to get that impression."

"Good." With a satisfied look in his eyes, Garth took her hand again and started down the stairs.

Seven

An hour into the huge backyard barbecue Devon knew Rita Dennison could safely relax. Everyone had shown up, and the lawn behind the Dennisons' newly built home was filled with chatting, laughing neighbors. When she got the chance, Devon caught Rita alone for a few minutes in the kitchen and congratulated her.

"The party's a success and your house is absolutely lovely, Rita," Devon assured her new friend.

Rita gave a relieved laugh. "I think you had something to do with the success of the barbecue. As soon as word got out that you and Garth would both be here and that you two were going to be married in a couple of weeks, nothing could have kept everyone in a fifty-mile radius from showing up tonight. I had no idea the two of you were such an item."

Devon wrinkled her nose. "You know how people love to gossip. Especially people in small communities. Here, let me help you carry those salads out to the buffet table."

"Thanks. These bowls are heavy. I spent all day yesterday making food. If I'd known what I was getting into when I invited everyone, I'd have thought twice." Rita handed Devon a huge platter of potato salad. "How many people are you going to be feeding at your reception?"

"I'm planning on two hundred. But I'll have Bev Middleton to help with the preparation," Devon said as she started out of the kitchen toward the long buffet table that had been set up on the lawn. "You and Sam will be coming, won't you?"

"Are you kidding? Wouldn't miss it for the world. Neither would anyone else I've spoken to lately."

A suntanned overly made-up woman in her late forties with badly bleached blond hair who'd been about to enter the house stopped as Devon came through the kitchen door. It was obvious at once that she had overheard the last few words. She gave Devon an arch look.

"Ah, the bride-to-be. Rita's absolutely correct, Devon. No one around here is going to miss your wedding. I'd heard you were back but until the invitation arrived in the mail yesterday I couldn't believe you were going to stay. Thought sure we'd seen the last of you when you left town for the big city."

"Hello, Mrs. Springer," Devon said coolly. "Nice to see you again." It wasn't, really, but it was inevitable, given the size of the community. Martha Springer and her husband ran the feed and grain store in Hawk Springs. When Devon's parents had been killed, one of the many debts left owing was the one to Springer Feed and Grain.

Devon's memories of Martha Springer's predictions about Lee and Kurt coming to a bad end were not pleasant ones. The older woman had lost no opportunity in the past to point out what an inadequate job Devon was doing of raising her two brothers. When both Lee and Kurt had been safely launched in college, Martha Springer had shrugged and declared it was just luck and the intervention of Garth Saxon. Everyone knew how Garth had stepped in and taken Lee in hand.

Rita glanced from one woman to the other and seemed to sense the unpleasant undercurrents between them. "If you were looking for the powder room, Mrs. Springer, it's just inside and down the hall to the left."

"Thank you. Frankly, I was looking for Devon. Haven't had a chance to speak to her since she returned to town."

"Maybe we could chat later, Mrs. Springer. I've got to help Rita with these salads."

"Oh, here, I'll give you a hand." Martha Springer stepped inside the kitchen and picked up a bowl. She hurried after the two younger women, catching up with them just as they reached the outside table. "You know, everyone's very curious about this whirlwind marriage you're planning, Devon. Kind of a quickie, isn't it?"

"Hardly a whirlwind affair, Mrs. Springer," Devon said smoothly as she positioned her salad bowl. "Garth asked me to marry him a year ago and I said yes at that time. We decided then to wait a year."

"I had no idea," Mrs. Springer pressed on determinedly. "I mean, Garth did mention occasionally that he'd be bringing you back from the city one of these days, but I just assumed you were long gone. You never seemed very happy here in Hawk Springs after you came back from college."

Devon saw Garth glance toward the buffet table and frown. He turned briefly back to the cluster of men with whom he'd been talking, excused himself and then started striding toward Devon. Perhaps he thought she needed rescuing. Devon smiled in amusement.

"I think we'll put all the salads at this end of the table with the bread in the middle," Rita was saying brightly in an obvious effort to cut through Martha Springer's determined chatter. "If you wouldn't mind carrying a few more things from the kitchen, Devon, I could certainly use the help."

"I'll be glad to give you a hand," Devon remarked, wondering why both Rita and Garth seemed suddenly determined to rescue her from Martha Springer. Devon had known the older woman for years and had a fair idea of what to expect.

"Excuse us, Mrs. Springer," Rita said firmly, stepping around the other woman.

"I'll be glad to help carry out a few more things, too," Mrs. Springer declared, refusing to let her quarry escape. "Tell me, Devon, how was San Francisco?"

"It's a wonderful city, Mrs. Springer."

"I hear Lee and Kurt are doing all right finally in college?"

"I know how much you worried about the future of my brothers, Mrs. Springer, so I'm sure you must be pleased to know they're doing just great." Out of the corner of her eye Devon saw that Garth was almost on them. She wondered exactly what he intended to do.

"Well, of course, everyone who knew about you and your brothers worried, Devon," Mrs. Springer said smoothly. "It was no secret that money was tight and heaven knows you had some problems. You were so young to be taking on the responsibility of two boys in their teens. I expect it must be a great relief to be finally marrying Garth Saxon." She paused for effect and then said in a voice that was loud enough to catch the attention of those standing nearby, "Now, at least, you won't have to worry about money anymore, will you?"

Rita's mouth thinned in quiet anger and Devon finally realized why her new friend had been trying to evade the older woman. Devon knew Martha Springer well enough to realize the woman had undoubtedly been giving anyone who would listen her opinion about the reasons for the marriage between Garth and Devon. In her infinite wisdom, Martha Springer had decided Devon must be marrying Garth for his money.

It stunned Devon to realize that she hadn't been expecting an attack from that side. All those years alone raising Lee and Kurt she'd been so proud, so determined not to ask for financial help from anyone in the community, least of all Garth. Didn't this foolish woman understand that money was the last reason Devon would marry? A wave of cold anger pulsed through her. She turned on Martha Springer.

But she was too late. Garth had already arrived on the scene. He glided to a halt behind Mrs. Springer in time to hear the woman's triumphant question.

"Martha," he drawled, startling the woman into whirling around in astonishment, "the really great thing about you is that you're consistent. Everyone in the area can rely on you to put your foot in your mouth at any given moment, day or night. You have a real talent for it, don't you?"

There were several amused grins from people who'd been standing nearby and who'd caught Mrs. Springer's comments to Devon.

Martha Springer turned red beneath her tan. "I don't know what you're talking about, Garth. I was just chatting with Devon and I—"

"Oh, we all know you've always had Devon's best interests at heart, Martha. Believe me, everyone here remembers how helpful you were in giving her advice about Lee and Kurt. You never lost an opportunity to tell her what she was doing wrong, did you?" Some of the grins on the faces of the surrounding people turned to chuckles and Martha Springer grew more red in the face.

"Now see here, Garth Saxon. I've known Devon most of her life."

"Then you must know she's one of the few women around who wouldn't marry for money. Hell, if I thought I could have gotten her to say yes that easily, I'd have shelled out the necessary cash a year ago. I'm always willing to put money into a good investment. But I'm sure you must realize just how proud Devon is when it comes to money. After all, she paid off every last dime her father owed you, didn't she?"

"Now hold on, Garth..."

"Speaking of money, we all know just how generous you were after her parents were killed, don't we? I wasn't here at the time, but I've heard how you didn't even bother to give Devon a little extra time to pay off the feed and grain tab at your store. You insisted on being paid on time. No extra credit. You've got a hell of a nerve claiming to be an old friend of the family. Good friends come through with more than advice when the chips are down."

There was outright laughter in the group that had gathered to hear the rest of the confrontation. Everyone in the area knew that Martha Springer hadn't offered anyone a dime in her life. The woman glanced around the circle of acquaintances in growing horror. She was suddenly the center of some very unwelcome attention.

Devon began to realize just how bad the scene could get. Garth was out for blood now, whether poor Mrs. Springer

realized it or not. He was a long way from the coup de
grace and he intended to make his victim suffer as much as
possible before he delivered the final blow. Rita looked
torn between wanting to see the older woman taken down
a notch and the fear of having her first major party ruined by an embarrassing confrontation. The crowd standing around the combatants was turning bloodthirsty as
only people in a small, closely knit community can. Martha Springer deserved what she was getting and her neighbors were more than happy to see her get it.

Devon drew a steadying breath. It was time to interrupt
the sport before it turned any bloodier. "I'm sure Mrs.
Springer felt her advice was worth a great deal more than
solid gold," Devon murmured dryly to an accompanying
round of laughter.

Garth glanced at her, his eyes gleaming. "Maybe, but we
all know how the value of gold has dropped during the past
few years," he said coolly.

The laughter grew keener and Devon was divided between exasperation and despair. "Mrs. Springer always
means well," she said, blandly dismissing the older woman
with an unconscious ease that would have been hard to
manage a year ago. "I've been looking for you, Garth.
Rita needs someone to take a load of charcoal out to Sam.
Would you mind?"

Garth hesitated, clearly not wanting to be deprived of his
victim, but Martha Springer was already slipping away into
the crowd, her face still burning with embarrassment. The
punishment wouldn't end here and everyone knew it. This
little scene would be rehashed a hundred times during the
coming week. Garth realized the game was over and
shrugged.

"Sure," he said, coming up the steps into the kitchen.
"I'll give you a hand with the charcoal." The screen door

slammed behind him, shutting off the attentive onlookers, who began to drift away as they realized the show was over.

"Honestly, Garth," Devon muttered as she stood facing him in the middle of the kitchen, "your social skills are a little rusty, aren't they? That was turning into quite a scene out there."

"Martha Springer deserved it," Rita said forcefully as she picked up another tray of salad. "I'm glad Garth arrived when he did. That woman's been asking for it ever since she heard you were back in town, Devon. She has an awfully big mouth."

"Devon knows that. She suffered enough from it when she was living in town with her brothers." Garth helped himself to a cracker he found on a platter and bit into it with strong, white teeth. The cracker crunched loudly and disappeared. "I don't want her at the wedding, Devon."

Devon cleared her throat. "It's too late, Garth. I already sent out the invitation."

"Cancel it."

"Well, that's a little easier said than done," she began delicately. "It would be much simpler to just let the invitation stand. Maybe she won't show up."

"Make sure she doesn't show up."

"Now, Garth, be reasonable, how can I do that?"

"If you can't find a way to do it, I will." He turned to Rita. "Where's the charcoal you want me to deliver to Sam?"

Rita glanced nervously at Devon. "I'm afraid there isn't any. Sam's already got the bags of charcoal."

Garth cocked a brow at Devon. "I see."

Devon blushed. "I just wanted to end things out there before they got too embarrassing. This is Rita's party, Garth. I don't want to be responsible for causing a major catastrophe.'' She sought for a way of changing the conversation. "Where's Ryan?"

"The last time I saw him, he and Ordway were talking to a bunch of local ranchers about computerizing their accounts. They weren't getting very far."

"I don't think they will," Rita put in comfortably. "At least, not as long as that Mr. Ordway is part of the team. Folks around here know Ryan and trust him, but they don't seem to care for Ordway. I heard Sam and some of the other men talking about him earlier. No offense, Garth."

"None taken," Garth assured her easily. "Personally, I can't stand him either—a real hustler."

Devon shot Garth a quelling glance. "I'm sure he's not that bad. His main problem as far as the locals are concerned is that he's an outsider. A city man, instead of a neighbor."

"Believe me, Devon," Garth said, "Ordway's as sleazy as they come. I'll bet Royal Standard's next stud fee that the only reason Ordway bothered to accept Ryan's invitation to come here tonight is because he's going to make a few last-ditch efforts to drum up some business before giving up and heading back to L.A. The guy never stops trying to sell. He should be working on a used car lot somewhere."

Devon narrowed her eyes, but said nothing. The last thing she wanted to do was start an argument. But secretly she felt a little sorry for Ryan's friend. Maybe Phil Ordway was a hustler, but chances were he was simply an upwardly mobile, hardworking young businessman trying to secure financial backing. It wasn't Ordway's fault that Hawk Springs automatically looked askance at outsiders, especially flashy outsiders who arrived in Porsches. She picked up a bowl of salad and thrust it into Garth's hands.

"Here," Devon said, "as long as you're standing there, you might as well make yourself useful."

"Yes, ma'am." Garth took the salad bowl and obediently exited the kitchen.

Rita stared after him thoughtfully as he left. "You know, I do believe the assault on Mrs. Springer tonight was meant to be a warning."

"A warning?" Devon gave her friend a questioning glance.

"Sure. Garth was making it clear that anyone who wants to take a shot at you is going to have to go through him, first."

Devon turned slightly pink. "I'm sorry about that scene outside a few minutes ago, Rita."

Rita laughed. "Like I said, forget it. Martha Springer had it coming. And at least it will make certain my party gets talked about after it's over. Folks won't be able to claim they were bored."

Devon gave a rueful sigh and picked up a salad bowl. "Something tells me life with Garth Saxon is never going to be boring."

"Something tells me you're right," Rita agreed with a smile. "Whoever said life out here in the sticks was dull?"

An hour later everyone was sitting down at the picnic tables that had been set up on the lawn. Plates were loaded with salads, thick chunks of buttered bread and huge slabs of barbecued beef. Devon sat beside Garth at a table that quickly filled up with a friendly assortment of neighbors. Ryan and Phil Ordway were sitting at another table around which sat some of the daughters of the guests. There was much giggling and a lot of low-voiced conversation from the group. Apparently Ryan and Phil had given up trying to pitch their schemes to the local ranchers and farmers and had decided to enjoy themselves.

"We're so pleased you're back in town," one of the women sitting at Devon's table remarked to her. "I know you must be excited about the wedding. I was talking to Bev Middleton the other day and she tells me you're planning a big reception. What fun!"

Garth picked up his knife. "Fun is not exactly the word that comes to my mind when I think about this wedding."

A man sitting across from Garth guffawed loudly. "Your fun comes after the wedding, Garth. Haven't you figured that part out yet?"

"Don't pay any attention to Bill," one of the women advised. "He's on his fourth beer. Tell me something, Devon, are you and Garth going to start your family right away? Neither one of you is a youngster. Can't wait too long, can you?"

Devon's hand froze halfway to her mouth. It came as a devastating shock to realize that she and Garth had never talked about children. Of course Garth would want babies. It would be one of his reasons for marrying. And he'd already waited so long, Devon thought in anguish. Why hadn't he brought up the subject? Was he just assuming she would be as anxious as he to have children? For God's sake, why hadn't she brought up the subject herself? She must have been deliberately suppressing it. Perhaps in the shock of accepting the fact that she really was going to marry Garth, she'd concentrated too much on the immediate situation and ignored the long-term implications.

A kind of panic assailed Devon. When she thought of children all she could think about were the years she'd spent alone with Lee and Kurt. She'd already lived through all the problems, the terrors and the worries of raising two teenagers. How could she turn around and start all over again?

Garth's hand was suddenly resting on the small fist she'd made in her lap. His fingers were warm and strong and infinitely reassuring as he answered the woman's question about children.

"Don't you know," he said quite casually, "that a year ago Devon just finished raising a couple of kids the hard way? The last thing I'd do is rush her into having her own babies until she's good and ready."

There were murmurs of understanding from those listening. Devon clutched at Garth's hand under the table, holding it fiercely as she tried to thank him silently for the reprieve. She remained silent, and the conversation quickly went on to other topics.

But the subject wasn't going to just disappear, Devon knew. Sooner or later she would have to deal with it. She stared sightlessly down at her plate, still clinging to Garth's fingers, and forced herself to think about the fact that neither she nor Garth had taken any precautions the night he'd made love to her at her San Francisco flat. The passion between them had sprung up too quickly and overwhelmed them too suddenly. A year of hunger had fed the flames, leaving little room for rational thought.

She could be carrying his baby even now.

Garth tightened his hand on hers and Devon glanced up to find him watching her with a strange expression in his eyes. It was an odd combination of possessiveness and reassurance. And she knew in that moment that he, too, was thinking of the night in San Francisco.

Devon felt abruptly disoriented, as if her world had suddenly, subtly altered in some indefinable way.

Watching her from the corner of his eye, Garth was certain he knew what was happening inside Devon's head.

This past week she'd begun to forget that she'd viewed marriage to him as a trap. Or perhaps she'd merely begun to accept it. Garth wasn't sure which. All he cared about was that she'd stopped fighting it. The day they had argued over the furniture, he knew he'd won the main battle even though Devon assumed she was the victor.

But with the mention of babies, she'd once again become aware of the bars of the cage she was entering. He sensed the sudden tension in her slender figure as she sat beside him, and realized she was thinking of that night in San Francisco when they'd made love without taking any precautions. Was she now resenting him as well as the passion that had flared between them?

He'd been so starved for her, and a year's aching hunger had been driving him. It had been impossible to hold back when the wait had finally ended. Surely she understood that he hadn't been thinking as rationally and clearly as he should have been that night, especially when he'd realized she was going to drag her feet and argue about going back to Hawk Springs. The terrible, lonesome ache he'd thought was finally about to end had swamped him when she'd started to tell him why they shouldn't marry. He'd had to stake his claim on her then or lose his mind.

He wanted to tell her that if she was pregnant it would be different this time. This baby would be her own, not a teenage brother only a few years younger than herself. But maybe that didn't seem very different to her, Garth thought. Maybe all she could see was the trap of commitment taking shape around her.

He could hardly deny that trap. There could be no marriage without it, and Garth had already done everything he could to give her time to adjust to it. But he'd waited as long as possible.

Devon flinched under his hand and he realized how tightly he was clasping her fingers. A few minutes earlier she'd been clinging to him, but now he was practically chaining her. He forced himself to release her and go back to his food.

Later, he promised himself. He would have this out with her when they were alone. He'd let her know that while he was guilty of not taking proper precautions the other night, nothing had changed. If she wasn't already pregnant, he would be careful in the future, at least for a while. He would try to give her more time. But if she was carrying his baby, then that was how it was. She belonged to him and he would have to find ways to help her accept that and the baby.

What it really came down to, Garth thought grimly, was that he would have to find ways to help her accept the life he was constructing around her.

The evening wore on, the guests growing louder and more boisterous under the Dennisons' backyard lights. When the small country and western band Rita had hired began to play, there was no lack of eager dancers. The music added to the general, good-natured din and Devon found herself seeking a few minutes of peace and quiet.

When Garth got involved in an intent discussion with his neighbors about the merits of a small nearby ranch that was coming on the market, Devon slipped away to the outlying shadows of the big yard. It seemed to her that she'd been needing some time to think since that unnerving conversation about babies at the table.

She walked in silence for a few minutes, lifting her face to the balmy evening air. When she came to the fence of a small paddock she leaned against it, staring toward the stall on the other side. A horse's tail swished absently in the shadows and a floppy-eared dog trotted past Devon's feet to see if anyone had inadvertently left some barbecued beef lying unattended on a paper plate.

The scent of hay and alfalfa and ranch animals seemed comfortable and familiar tonight. Devon realized she'd lived with these earthy smells most of her life. They were intimately bound up with the routine of planting and harvesting, of calving and foaling, of tracking the weather with an anxious eye. They were part of the endless, intimate cycle of life lived close to the land.

Sometimes in the city one forgot what it was like to live this close to reality.

"Hey," said a familiar voice directly behind her, "you look a little bored. Can't say that I blame you."

Devon drew a breath and turned slowly around to find Phil Ordway approaching. She managed a smile. "Hello, Phil. Enjoying the evening?"

"It's an experience, I'll say that much for it." He shook his handsome head. His words were just faintly slurred. He took another swallow from the beer he was holding. "That music's enough to drive a man over a cliff. This beer is pure blue-collar and all anyone back there wants to talk about is land and crops and cows and horses."

"I guess people around here aren't ready for the wonders of the computer age yet," Devon said, feeling a little sorry for the man.

"You can say that again. They're all about fifty years behind the times. I don't see how you can stand this environment, Devon. You look like you'd have settled down just fine in San Francisco. What made you decide to come back here?"

"I grew up here." Devon shrugged. "Sometimes it's harder to get away than you'd expect."

"Hell, if I were you, I'd be long gone." Ordway came to stand beside her in the darkness. He rested one elbow on a fence rail and looked down at her. "Ryan told me you're marrying Saxon in a couple of weeks."

"That's right." The smell of beer on his breath was annoying. Devon wondered just how much he'd had to drink.

"I can't imagine why," Ordway said angrily. "The guy's living in the dark ages. If you don't watch out, he'll drag you back into them, too."

Devon stirred uneasily, aware of the bitterness in Phil's voice. He was clearly still smarting from his failure to convince Garth to back him and Ryan. "Garth's a little old-fashioned in some ways," she admitted, trying to be diplomatic. She understood some of Ordway's resentment. This trip had been a total waste of time for him.

"A little old-fashioned! That's putting it mildly," Ordway told her derisively. "You should have heard him this afternoon when I tried to explain our financial proposal to him. He isn't willing to take any risks at all."

"He has to be very convinced of the merits of a project before he'll commit to it," Devon explained gently. "He never rushes into things."

"He's just a dumb hick rancher who can't tell a prospectus from a stock option."

"Excuse me," Devon said coolly, her brief sympathy fading at once. "I think I'd better be getting back to the others." She turned to go but Ordway caught her wrist, pulling her to a halt. When she glanced back uneasily she saw that his expression was harsh and resentful.

"Why are you rushing back to the cowboy? Going to bed with him must be about as exciting for you as heating up a can of beans. I'll bet he knows more about riding a horse than he does about what makes a woman happy in bed. You could do a whole lot better than him."

Devon began to grow uneasy. It occurred to her that Phil Ordway was more intoxicated than she'd originally guessed. She tried to free her wrist and discovered the man had locked his fingers around it. "Mr. Ordway, please let me go," she said very firmly.

"I'm leaving for L.A. tonight," he told her a little thickly. "I told Ryan a few minutes ago that I'm not wasting any more time here in this burg. I'd be willing to do you a favor and take you with me. You don't belong here in Hawk Springs any more than I do. I can tell that just by looking at you."

"Let me go," Devon repeated, beginning to wonder if she was going to be able to end this without causing an embarrassing scene. "You've had a little too much to drink and you're angry because you couldn't sell your idea to Garth, but that's no reason for you to act this way."

"That cowboy would be madder than hell if I took you back to Los Angeles with me, wouldn't he? Serve him right. It would really teach him a lesson."

"Phil, stop it."

He forced her closer. "Yeah, it would serve him right. Nothing like running off with a man's woman to teach him he's out of his league. You're gonna like L.A., Devon. And I can guarantee I'm gonna be a whole lot more interesting in bed than that cowboy. Come here and I'll give you a sample."

Devon couldn't believe this was happening. The situation had abruptly escalated out of control. She opened her mouth to shout for assistance, simultaneously bringing her free hand up in a fist aimed at Ordway's jaw.

But he yanked fiercely on her wrist, causing her to stumble. She fell to the grass and found Ordway's hand across her mouth. Frantically she struggled in silence, kicking and clawing as Ordway tried to pin her to the ground.

"Stop it, you little spitfire. You don't know how good it's going to be. I'll show you what you've been missing. I'll also show Saxon just how stupid he is. Damn you!" This last came as Devon raked her nails across his cheek.

Devon saw the fury in Ordway's eyes and tried desperately to push him off of her. She was scrabbling in the grass for a rock or a stick or anything that could be used as a weapon when she was suddenly free. Ordway's weight was abruptly gone. She knew who her rescuer was even before she raised her eyes to his face.

"Garth!"

She struggled for breath as she watched Phil Ordway being dragged to his feet. Before she found her tongue, Garth calmly slammed a large fist into Ordway's jaw.

The man crumpled to the ground.

Eight

Two hours later Garth sprawled in majestic solitude in the sanctity of his study. He was leaning back in his chair, jacket off, collar undone, his booted feet on the desk, one fist wrapped around a glass of whiskey. The Stetson was on the couch where he'd thrown it earlier when he'd slammed into the room and shut the door behind him.

He was in a blisteringly savage mood and the whole household knew it.

The members of that household had done what members of households have traditionally done when the master is in a roaring temper. They had discreetly retreated from sight. Even the dogs had vanished after a quick, loud greeting. Bev Middleton had murmured good-night and hurried upstairs to bed as soon as Garth had stalked into the living room where she was innocently watching TV. Devon had made one weak effort to say something to Garth, but after taking a look at his face in the hall light she'd changed her mind and followed Bev up the stairs. An hour ago Ryan had returned from his task of dumping Ordway into a room at the motel on the edge of town. He hadn't paused to consult with Garth, but had retreated to his bedroom. The house was absolutely silent now and Garth had the entire downstairs to himself.

He used the isolation and the silence to contemplate the full extent of his anger. The fury he'd felt toward Ordway was still burning in him. The single blow Garth had gotten in before the rest of the guests descended on the scene hadn't been nearly enough to work off the hot rage that had exploded when he'd realized what the man was doing to Devon.

Garth would have preferred to take Phil Ordway apart limb by limb but that proved impossible, not only because a hundred people had converged on the combatants but because Devon was clinging to the fence rail looking shocked and stunned. The memory of her eyes, huge and pleading in the moonlight, sent another jolt of anger through Garth.

This time the anger was directed at himself. He took a swallow of whiskey and wondered just how much had been put at risk tonight. He'd never seen Devon look at him like that. He could just imagine what she'd been thinking. No doubt she'd been comparing him to her soft, gentlemanly city friends. Her expression had made it clear she hadn't fully realized just how uncivilized, uncultured and uncouth her future husband was until that moment.

He knew Devon had been viewing her coming marriage as a trap, one she was prepared to enter gingerly and somewhat reluctantly. Garth had been coaxing her in the direction he wanted her to go, using her year-old promise and her sense of commitment to prod her. His mouth tightened as he examined the toe of his boot through narrowed eyes. After tonight's violence Devon would no longer be just mildly skittish about the future he'd planned for her. She would probably try to abandon it altogether. He wondered when and where she would run.

Then he started wondering what she would do when he came after her. For as sure as hell, he would go after her.

Upstairs in her bedroom Devon paced barefoot across the carpet in front of the bed. The house had been unnaturally quiet since Ryan had returned. She knew Garth was still downstairs because she'd been listening intently for the sound of his footsteps in the hall. There hadn't even been a squeak from the floorboards. Was he going to spend the whole night down there?

Devon paused in front of the window and stood staring out into the darkness. She was feeling a bit calmer now. The initial shock had passed, but she still felt oddly restless and uneasy. It was as if some of the adrenaline was still flowing in her veins, seeking an outlet.

If her own body was reacting this strongly in the aftermath of the traumatic events, she could only imagine what Garth must be feeling. The rage she'd seen burning in his eyes had been frightening. She remembered wanting to run into his arms and had found herself clinging to the fence for support, instead. No woman in her right mind went into the arms of a man whose eyes had glazed the way Garth's had after he'd flattened Ordway.

It had struck her then that Garth probably blamed her for having allowed herself to get into the ugly situation in the first place. Some, perhaps most, of the anger she'd seen in him had been directed at her.

Devon shivered and turned away from the window. She stood staring for a moment at the closed door of her room and tried to imagine what Garth was thinking.

Damn it, he had no right to blame her for what had happened.

Perhaps now that he'd had a chance to calm down she would point that fact out to him, Devon thought. Impulsively, she opened her door and went out into the hall. She was still wearing the clothes she'd worn to the barbecue except for her shoes and panty hose. Her bare feet made no sound on the stairs as she descended into the darkness below.

There was a sliver of light beneath the study door but no sound came from inside. Devon hesitated and then put her hand on the doorknob. Cautiously she pushed open the door.

Garth's eyes met hers instantly, although he didn't move from where he lounged in dangerous stillness behind the desk. The desk lamp illuminated his booted feet resting on the polished wood surface but left his face in intimidating shadow. She glanced at the drink in his hand as she quietly came into the room and shut the door behind her.

"So," Garth said, far too evenly, "one member of the household finally got up enough nerve to come downstairs." He took a swallow from his glass.

Devon stood where she was, her hands wrapped around the doorknob behind her back. She decided she needed the support. "You have to admit you were in an awesomely foul mood when we came home from the party."

"I was madder than hell."

"Yes, I got that feeling. Are you still angry or has the whiskey had some soothing effect?" Very carefully she came away from the door and went to stand in front of the desk.

"I haven't had enough whiskey to do much good yet. But I'm working on it."

"So I see."

He regarded her narrowly. "Just chalk it up to that long list you're making."

"What long list?"

"The one that has all my uncivilized manners, my unsophisticated, rural attitudes and my bad temper itemized on it."

"Oh, that list." She nodded wryly.

"What are you doing here, Devon?"

She shrugged. "What am I doing here at the ranch? You should know. You're the one who brought me here."

He slammed the empty whiskey glass down on the desk. "Damn it, don't play games with me tonight. I'm not in the mood for it. Why did you come downstairs?"

She saw the challenging glitter in his eyes and wondered at it. "I came down here to inform you that what happened tonight was not my fault and that I don't think it's fair of you to blame me. I resent it."

He blinked slowly and slid his boots off the desk. Then he got to his feet with an almost lazy movement. His eyes never left her face. "You think I'm blaming you?"

"That was the impression I got, yes." She faced him defiantly, refusing to back away from his overwhelming presence. She still had the desk between herself and Garth. That should give her some protection.

He appeared to be contemplating her remark as though the whole idea were new to him. "I suppose an objective observer might say I had reason to blame you for what happened at the Dennisons' tonight."

"Now, Garth . . ."

"After all," he continued ruthlessly, "it was your idea to invite Ordway to the ranch, wasn't it? Give him a chance, you said. Listen to what Ordway and Ryan have to say. Let them have a fair hearing. Maybe Ordway really knows what he's doing. Maybe he's a nice guy who will make Ryan an excellent business partner. Think about backing him financially."

Devon coughed. "Garth, you know I didn't say all that."

"Maybe not those exact words, but the end result was the same, wasn't it? Ordway shows up and the next thing I know, he's attacking my fiancée."

Devon's eyes widened. "It would never have gotten very far. For heaven's sake, Garth, there were nearly fifty people within shouting distance."

"But you weren't shouting."

Devon felt her own temper slipping. She'd come down here intending to be calm and firm and rational. Instead, she was starting to react to the aggression and frustrated hostility that was emanating from Garth. "I couldn't shout! He had his hand over my mouth."

"Why in hell did you let him get that close?"

"He just came over to where I was standing by the fence and started talking," Devon explained furiously. "He'd had too much to drink and he was very upset about the failure of his plans. He felt you hadn't given him a fair hearing."

"So he decided he'd take a little revenge on me by roughing up my woman?" Garth said very softly.

"It didn't start out that way," Devon tried to say. "He just started talking about taking me back to L.A. with him tonight. He said he thought I belonged there instead of here and he'd be glad to give me a lift."

"That piece of slime! I should have broken his neck. What the hell did you say when he made this grand offer to save you from marrying a cowboy?"

"Garth, please, you're getting irrational."

"Wrong. I was feeling irrational before you even walked through that door. I'm way beyond irrational now. *What did you say when he offered to take you away with him?*"

"I tried to excuse myself and return to the party."

"Tried to excuse yourself? Well, how delightfully civilized of you, Miss Ellwood. Just gave him a polite little smile and tried to excuse yourself, huh?"

"Damn it, Garth, I was trying to avoid a scene!"

"Anything to avoid a scene. Hell, yes. Mustn't have a scene. How far were you prepared to go to avoid an embarrassing *scene*, Devon?"

She paled and then the color surged back into her face as her fury skyrocketed. "What, exactly, are you implying Garth? That I would have let myself deliberately get mauled by Ordway just to avoid a scene?"

"All I know for sure is that you *were* getting mauled by Ordway when I found you." He came around the end of the desk in a swift, predatory movement that had Devon instinctively stepping backward out of the way. But he didn't stop until she found herself against the wall—literally and figuratively. Then he planted his large hands against the paneling on either side of her head, trapping her. "You know what, Devon? It didn't look to me like you were enjoying yourself."

"I wasn't!"

"Why not? Ordway's a nice, sophisticated city boy. He must know all the right moves. What went wrong?"

"Don't you dare imply I welcomed his advances. He was assaulting me, Garth!"

"Yeah, that's the impression I got, too. I saw the marks you left on his face."

"Then stop accusing me."

"Were you a little bit tempted by his offer of a lift to L.A., Devon?"

"No, damn it!"

"Are you sure? Didn't you start thinking about city lights and sophisticated apartments and Porsches and singles bars?"

"What are you trying to do, Garth?" she hissed.

"I'm trying to find out the truth. I want to know how close you are to running. I want to know if you're starting to panic and feel that there's a trap closing around you."

"Is that how you want me to think of marriage to you? As a trap?"

"Why not?" he demanded aggressively. "It will be, won't it? Think about it. You'll be stuck here at Hawk's Flight most of the time. You won't have many opportunities to wear your fancy city dresses and high heels. You'll be up at dawn and in bed at an early hour. *My* bed. And one of these days there'll be babies."

She flinched, not at the deliberate threat, but at the way he said it. "Is that right? You're going to accomplish that last bit all by yourself?"

"No, Devon, you're going to be right there with me, every step of the way. That's how it works out here, remember? A man and his wife work together. And they make babies together."

"I don't need an elementary sex lesson."

"Are you sure? Have you realized you might already be pregnant?"

She stared up at him. "It occurred to me this evening, yes."

"I know. I saw the look on your face. Was that why you wandered away from the rest of us, Devon?" he asked bitterly. "Were you suddenly realizing just how trapped you might already be?"

"Why do you keep using that word?" she flung back at him.

"Trapped? Because that's the way you see yourself." He dropped his hands to her shoulders and pulled her abruptly close. "And God help me," he breathed, "it's not far from the truth. I *have* trapped you, Devon. Now that I've finally got you, I'm going to keep you. Don't ever try to run from me. I swear I'll come after you and bring you home. You belong here, Devon, whether you realize it or not. One of these days you'll understand."

"Will I?" But the words were left half said as he brought his mouth down on hers. Devon felt the shudder of masculine need and anticipation that went through Garth and her simmering anger began to metamorphose into something else. Her lips parted beneath the punishing, demanding kiss.

The frustrated fury that had been burning in Garth was quickly translating itself into a relentless passion that had the momentum of an avalanche behind it. Devon responded, her senses leaping to match his as he pinned her against the hard length of his body.

"Remember this," Garth said thickly as he tangled his hands in her hair. "Remember how you come alive in my arms the next time some city dude invites you to run off with him."

"I wasn't even thinking of running off, Garth." She wrapped her arms around his neck and looked up at him with eyes that were beginning to glow with the passion only he could elicit. "What's more, I resent the implication that I would run off with someone like Phil Ordway. I want an apology."

"Do you?" Garth slid his hands down to her throat. "Well, come and get your apology, Devon."

"I'd like to make you offer it on your knees," she vowed tightly.

"Feeling vengeful?" He found the laces of her tunic.

"Yes, as a matter of fact. You've been in a vicious temper since that scene with Ordway and I think you owe everyone in the house an apology."

"Is that right?" He pulled the laces free with quick, snapping movements.

"Yes, that's right."

"Then come here and see what you can do to convince me to make a full-scale, public apology." He whipped the tunic off over her head and his hands went to her satin-covered breasts. He unsnapped the clip of the bra.

"This isn't a good way to settle an argument, Garth," Devon tried to say as he discarded the bra and slid his palms down her waist to remove her skirt.

"No?"

"No. You're angry and aroused and you're not thinking clearly. We should talk."

"I don't know about angry and I don't know how clearly I'm thinking, but I sure as hell am aroused. I want you so badly I ache. We'll talk later." He had her skirt off now. He let it fall to the floor as he slipped his fingers inside the waistband of her panties.

Devon trembled as she felt his strong hands cup her buttocks and squeeze her with slow, deep pleasure. She sighed and nestled her head against his chest. Then she felt him move his arms around her, lifting her. She closed her eyes as he carried her over to the sofa and put her down on the cushions.

When she heard the rustle of his clothing, she opened her eyes to watch him undress. As the last of his garments fell to the floor she found herself staring at the bold, hard lines of his body.

"What's the matter, Devon?" he asked a little roughly as he sat down beside her on the couch. "You're not afraid of me, are you?"

"No. But you *can* be intimidating. I've told you that before."

"I get the feeling I don't intimidate you as much as I should." He groaned as he leaned down to kiss her breast. His tongue touched her in a deliberate caress that made her shiver in his arms. "Maybe if I were better at it, I wouldn't have to rescue you from men like Ordway. You'd exercise a bit more caution."

"So now you see yourself as having conducted a rescue operation? A while ago you were practically accusing me of planning to run off with him." She braced her hand against his shoulder, trying to hold him away from her while she berated him. Her emotions were still a wild mixture of passion and resentment and love.

"Hush, Devon. I don't want to talk about it anymore. Not now." He caught her wrist and put her hand around his neck so that she could no longer restrain him. The hair on his chest teased her nipples as he leaned over her, one heavy thigh trapping her legs.

"Just because you don't feel like talking about the subject is no reason to try to halt the conversation. As it happens, I think we should talk about it. We have a serious problem here, Garth. One that needs to be resolved."

"The only problem we have at the moment is your mouth. Fortunately, I know how to handle it." He kissed her deeply, sliding his tongue between her lips to challenge and tease and finally dominate.

Devon moaned, surrendering to the sweet, intoxicating passion that was ensnaring her. She tightened her hands on Garth and as he felt her yielding response he groaned in soft satisfaction.

"Touch me, Devon. I've got to feel your hands on me." His own hands were moving slowly and caressingly on her, gliding down over her hips and trailing up the inside of her thighs.

Devon stirred under his touch, her whole body igniting. She sank her nails into his hard buttocks in a convulsive little gesture of excitement that seemed to arouse him even more than he already was. He found her questing fingers and guided them downward.

"I don't know what gave you the idea you aren't sufficiently intimidating," Devon complained throatily, as she closed her fingers around him. She stroked him gently, reveling in the shape and feel of him. He was big and powerful and her body tingled with vivid awareness of him.

Garth's husky chuckle was muffled against her shoulder. "There are times, Devon, when you are very good for my ego." He used his teeth in a very careful, very sexy manner that made Devon melt against him.

"Garth?"

"Do you want me, Devon?"

"You know I do." She moved her legs invitingly, urging him closer.

"I need to hear you say it. I'll probably never be able to hear it often enough." He probed gently between her thighs until she writhed against him.

"I want you, Garth. Please."

"Aren't I pleasing you?" He was playing with her, tormenting her and exciting her without mercy. He seemed to know exactly how to touch her to make her go up in flames.

"Yes, yes, you're pleasing me," she gasped, closing her thighs tightly around his hand because she needed more of him. "But I can't stand the waiting. Come here, Garth."

"Soon."

"No, now."

"Do you know what you do to me when you respond like this?" he whispered against her throat.

"Tell me." She opened her eyes to gaze up at him with a dazed excitement. Her whole body was throbbing with need. She loved him so much, she thought. She wondered if he had any idea of just how strong her emotions were and immediately decided he undoubtedly did. Garth was a very astute man. He would know when he held a woman in the palm of his hand.

"I'll do better than that," he promised. "I'll show you what you do to me." He released her briefly to pull away and reach for his pants.

"What are you doing?" she asked, suddenly alarmed.

"Taking the precautions I should have taken last time." There was a soft rustling sound in the shadows and then Garth came back to her. "If you're already pregnant, then this is a waste of time. But if you aren't, I don't want to take any more chances until we're ready to make that kind of decision."

"Precautions?" She ignored everything else he said, concentrating on the one fact that amazed her. "You're prepared tonight? Down here in your study? But, Garth..."

"Don't look so shocked," he teased softly. "I've been carrying the necessities around in my wallet since that night in San Francisco." He moved to cover her body with his own. "I didn't want to take any more chances. I wanted you to feel safe."

"But I thought you didn't intend to make love to me again until we got married." She clung to his shoulders as he lay heavily against her.

"I didn't intend to do this again until we got married because I didn't think I'd have a chance. Not with Bev and

Ryan in the house. But I'm learning that around you, sweetheart, my most brilliant plans sometimes go astray."

She smiled dreamily up at him. "I'm glad."

"So am I," he admitted. And then he was slowly, steadily pushing himself into her.

Devon felt the hardness of him as he sank into her softness and she cried out in a little gasp of pleasure and acceptance. He drank the sound from her lips, swallowing it before it had a chance to escape the confines of the room.

Garth watched Devon's face as he took her completely. He was throbbing with the tension it took to control himself, but he refused to give in to the pull of her sweet passion just yet. There were too many other things he wanted to revel in first. He needed to see the way she lost control and gave herself to him totally. He wanted to glory in the sensation of her tight, satiny body. She was so perfect, so right for him. He wondered if she understood that. If she did, perhaps she wouldn't daydream about city life and city nights. She would know he needed her.

"Oh, Garth, I can't stand any more of this." She dug her nails into his back, trying to force him to increase the slow, deliberate rhythm he had established.

Garth wanted to laugh with satisfaction and triumph as he felt her frantic but useless efforts to make him hurry. "This is too good to rush, sweetheart. Take it easy."

"I can't take it easy."

"Do you want to take over?" he asked, nibbling at her earlobe. Meanwhile he never ceased the steady, pulsing beat.

"Yes, please," she begged. "I can't stand the waiting."

"All right. It's your turn." He stilled his movements, pulling free of her. Then he deftly reversed their positions on the narrow couch. When Devon opened her eyes she was lying on top of him. He saw the momentary confusion mixed with the cloudy passion in her gaze and wanted to laugh again. She was a total delight to all his senses. "I'm waiting," he drawled. He held her by the waist, steadying her as she reoriented herself.

"Oh, good," she managed breathlessly. "Now I can show you how it should be done."

He grinned. "You do that, little witch."

But she was already fumbling around, fitting herself to him with a sweet awkwardness that didn't lessen the mounting excitement in the least. If anything, Garth decided, her uncertain movements combined with her overwhelming determination to take charge was an almost unbearable stimulation to his already inflamed senses. "Hurry," he growled as she struggled with the unfamiliar position.

"Now look who's begging." She finally found her balance and carefully eased herself down onto him. Her hands splayed across his chest and her eyes were very wide as she adjusted herself. "This is very nice," she finally said, not moving.

"I agree." He stroked her thighs, enjoying the feel of her astride him. "You can set the pace now."

"Yes." She still didn't move.

"What's wrong?" he asked softly as she just sat there, staring down at him.

"Nothing's wrong."

"I thought you wanted things to move a little faster."

"I did," she said with a sparkling innocence that didn't fool him for a minute. "But now I'm seeing all sorts of possibilities."

"Devon . . ."

"I think that if I'm very careful, very controlled and exercise all sorts of willpower, I could just sit here all night. A sort of Zen approach to sex."

"I didn't realize you had such a vengeful streak in you."
Garth shifted abruptly, lifting her up and off of him.

"Wait, Garth..." she began hurriedly as she felt herself losing control of the situation. "I was only teasing."

"This," he informed her as he eased her off the couch and down onto the floor where he could move more freely, "is what happens to women who like to tease." He pinned her wrists and parted her legs again. Then he entered her without hesitation. Instantly she tightened around him, clinging to him as her hair spilled around her on the rug.

"I'll have to be sure to try it more often," she murmured.

"Any time," he invited. Then his own need took control of both of them. There was no more teasing, no more talk, no more enticements or pleas. There was only the pounding, surging, reckless desire that drove them both toward the brink.

And then they were both sailing over the edge, clutching each other in an unshakable embrace. At the last instant, Garth heard the cry that threatened to escape Devon as her passion went out of control. Quickly he moved to seal it behind her lips, distantly mindful of the two people sleeping upstairs. When his own release shook him to the core he buried his mouth against Devon's shoulder, frantically struggling to muffle himself.

Afterward Devon lay quietly for a long time, trailing her fingertips over Garth's shoulders with absent pleasure as she came slowly out of the tranquil, relaxed aftermath. When he finally stirred and looked down at her she didn't know whether to laugh or groan at the sheer male contentment she saw in his gaze.

"Isn't this a bit outrageous for you, Garth?" she murmured daringly. "Not only have you taken to hiding contraceptives in your wallet, but when you finally do make love to me again we wind up all over the couch and down on the floor. We're nowhere near a proper bed. It's positively shocking.''

"You don't look shocked. You look like a sleek little cat who's just eaten a very large bowl of cream." He smiled down at her indulgently.

"Umm." She stretched and yawned delicately. "That's rather how I feel."

He lifted himself slightly away from her, watching her pert breasts move as she raised her arms over her head. Garth bent and kissed one rosy nipple. Then he glanced at the watch on his wrist. "It's late."

"I'm not surprised."

He reluctantly got to his feet. "You'd better hightail it up to bed." He reached down to scoop up her clothes and hand them to her. "Take it easy on the stairs. Don't make a sound. I don't want Bev or Ryan to hear you."

"Yes, Garth."

"Are you laughing at me, woman?"

"No, Garth."

His mouth twitched. "Uh-huh. We'll argue about it some other time. Right now I want you back in your bed where you belong. Move, sweetheart."

"Yes, Garth."

She did as she was told and climbed the stairs silently. Just as quietly she let herself into her room and closed the door. Then she fell into bed, grinning to herself in the darkness. There was something very endearing about the combination of old-fashioned virtues and passionate vices that characterized Garth Saxon. A exciting contradiction.

He worried excessively about her reputation and at the same time he had started carrying contraceptives in his wallet. He made love to her on the study couch and then hustled her upstairs to bed so that no one would guess what had transpired, even though they were going to be married in two weeks.

Devon heard the faintest of sounds outside her door and knew that Garth had just paused by her room before going to his own. The grin faded from her face as she remembered how dangerously angry he'd been earlier that evening. When she'd left him a few minutes ago there had been no trace of the fury that had precipitated the passionate scene in the study.

She'd soothed the savage beast with sex, Devon told herself. But she doubted if anything had really changed. Garth must know by now he had only to touch her and she responded. For her part, she had no doubts about the level of his commitment. His integrity, his honesty and his passion were indisputable. She should have no qualms.

The marriage would take place as planned, but deep inside, Devon wondered if commitment, integrity, honesty and even passion were enough. She wanted all those things, of course. But she also wanted love.

Garth had never said anything about love. Devon knew that because of his ex-wife and perhaps because of the kind of man he was, he didn't think in such ill-defined, vague terms. He was a practical man, Devon reminded herself. And he'd seen a woman who had claimed to love him leave on the arm of another man.

It was understandable that for Garth, love was not a particularly important or reliable part of the equation that equaled a good marriage.

Nine

Devon came downstairs the morning after the Dennisons' barbecue to find a very subdued kitchen crowd. Garth hadn't yet made an appearance and everyone else seemed to be hoping he'd put it off indefinitely.

Bev Middleton was stirring pancake batter with a brisk hand while she chatted in low tones to Steve and Cal. She gave Devon a sympathetic, almost worried glance and said good-morning. The two ranch hands appeared wary. They were drinking their ritual three cups of coffee but looked ready to depart the kitchen on short notice if necessary. Ryan was sitting hunched over at the breakfast table, nursing his own mug. It was obvious that all those present were prepared for the worst when Garth came downstairs. Clearly no one expected his temper to have improved overnight.

"Good morning, everyone," Devon said with a calm smile as she took a seat across from Ryan. The others mumbled greetings and looked more uneasy than ever. "I'll take some of that coffee, Ryan."

He hurried to pour her a cup. "Are you all right, Devon?" he asked quietly.

"I'm fine. Why shouldn't I be all right?"

Ryan's mouth hardened. "Because of that damned Phil Ordway."

"Ah." Devon nodded with understanding and tasted her coffee. "It was a bit messy for a while, but Garth took care of things in his usual inimitable style, didn't he?"

"I'm sorry, Devon," Ryan said urgently. "I swear, I had no idea Ordway was the kind of man who would pull something like that. It's all my fault he was here in the first place. Garth should have thrown a punch at me as well as Ordway."

"Don't be ridiculous," Devon said bluntly. "You are most definitely not responsible for what happened, and I won't have you blaming yourself. Who could have guessed what Ordway would be like when he'd had a few drinks in him?"

"You may not blame me," Ryan declared, "but it's a safe bet Garth will. What's more, he'll be right. I should have listened to him when he told me he didn't like the sound of Phil Ordway."

Steve glanced at Ryan. "We heard about the fight first thing this morning. It's the main topic of conversation down at the new barn."

"Also heard Garth was mad as hell," Cal added.

"He is," Bev assured them. "I saw his face when he came in last night dragging Devon behind him. Even the dogs ran for cover."

Steve shrugged, eyeing Devon. "Sounded like he had a right."

"Doesn't matter if he did," Cal said wryly. "He'll still be hell to work with today. I don't mind saying I'm not exactly looking forward to it."

Bev sighed. "He'll get over it. Eventually. He was like this for a while after Devon left last year. Just watch your step around him for a while. He'll be looking for someone to chew on till he works the anger out of his system."

Devon listened to the morose predictions with interest and wondered just how upset Garth had been those first weeks after she'd left for the city. She remembered that time very well, herself. There'd been the excitement of being free at last and the stress of finding an apartment and a job to occupy her, but there'd been a measure of unexpected loneliness to deal with, too. She recalled that the loneliness had surprised her. She hadn't expected to feel anything but unmitigated joy after finally leaving Hawk Springs.

"What's Ordway going to do?" Steve asked Ryan.

Ryan glanced at his watch. "My guess is he's already left town. I dumped him in the motel last night and left his keys where he'd see them first thing this morning."

"I wonder if he'll sue," Devon murmured.

"Are you kidding?" Ryan managed a trace of a sardonic smile. "He'd never stand a chance. Everyone at that party will swear he started the fight. Besides, he won't want to go through the embarrassment of pressing charges. His ego won't let him call attention to the fact that he got the worst of the mess. No, I think it's safe to say we've all seen the last of Phil Ordway."

It was Garth who startled everyone by responding to Ryan's comment. "Best news I've heard since we found out Royal Standard wasn't sterile," he announced easily as he sauntered into the kitchen. He appeared totally oblivious to the wary looks he was receiving from Bev, Ryan,

Steve and Cal. He nodded impartially, including all of them in the greeting. "'Morning, everyone. That coffee smells extra good today, Bev. I'll have about twenty of those pancakes."

He sat down next to Devon, giving her an unhurried, satisfied, intimate smile. Then he reached out to ruffle her hair with an absent, possessive affection that made the others stare. "I'd sell the south pasture for a cup of that coffee this morning."

Devon picked up the coffeepot and poured the rich brew into Garth's mug. "Good morning, Garth." She was aware of everyone else in the kitchen fumbling for low-voiced, cautious greetings. It was obvious they were all waiting for a continuation of last night's explosion—and equally obvious that the lack of it was confusing them.

Steve and Cal had half risen as if to escape and now sank slowly back into their chairs to finish their coffee. Garth leaned back and began talking calmly about the day's work he'd planned. He was relaxed and matter-of-fact about it. Steve and Cal listened and nodded attentively. Occasionally they cast speculative glances in Devon's direction. She pretended not to notice.

Bev set a large plate of pancakes down in front of Garth and looked mildly astonished when he thanked her warmly and dug into the food with gusto. Bev, too, gave Devon a curious look.

Ryan was the last one to relax in Garth's presence. It was plain he'd braced himself for a full-scale catastrophe and wasn't sure how to handle the reprieve. Devon took pity on him, and when Ryan opened his mouth to say something, she silently shook her head. Ryan closed his mouth again and took a swallow of his coffee. Then he, too, flicked her a speculative glance.

The lion dined with hearty pleasure, completely unaware of the cautious watchfulness of the rest of those present. When he'd finished his pancakes, he took a final taste of coffee and suggested it was time to go to work.

No one argued. Steve and Cal practically tripped over each other en route to the door. Ryan hastily gulped the rest of his coffee and jumped to his feet to follow the other men. Bev watched them all depart and then turned, hands on her hips, to survey Devon who sat alone at the table. The older woman grinned.

"Well, well, well," Bev said with deep interest.

Devon smiled breezily, pouring more coffee for herself. "Well what?"

"Well, aren't you the lady with the magic touch." Bev dropped into a chair and reached for the coffeepot. "A real miracle worker. Haven't seen that man look that pleased with himself since I can't remember when. 'Bout time he started living a normal life. Man like him wasn't meant to go without a woman in his bed. Lucky for the rest of us the two of you decided to finally get together last night. Couldn't have happened at a better time. I don't even want to think about what kind of mood Garth would have been in this morning if you hadn't gone downstairs to the study last night."

"Bev!" But Devon was torn between laughter and chagrin. "He'd explode if he thought you knew what had happened last night. How *did* you know, anyway? I was as quiet as a mouse on those stairs."

Bev's eyes twinkled. "I didn't hear you on the stairs. I took an educated guess about what must have happened based on the change in Garth's mood this morning. Only one thing on earth could have taken that snarling lion last night and turned him into a purring tomcat this morning. A woman's touch."

Devon shook her head, her mouth curving wryly. "Do you think everyone else around here will come to the same brilliant conclusion?"

"Yup. Doesn't take much in the way of brains to figure it out, I'm afraid. Does that worry you?"

"No," Devon said honestly. "But I'm not sure what Garth will do if he thinks everyone on the place has figured out what happened in the study last night."

"Well, we'll just have to hope the men have sense enough to keep their mouths shut. 'Course that might be hard for 'em to do. They're all so danged relieved. Everyone on the place was expecting Garth to be a walking mine field today. I don't need to tell you that by now most folks within fifty miles have probably heard about what happened at the Dennisons' barbecue last night."

"No," Devon agreed, "you don't need to tell me. News travels fast around here, doesn't it?"

"That it does." Bev sipped her coffee with satisfaction. "You want to go over the menu for the reception this morning?"

Devon nodded. "Definitely. I want to make all the final decisions on it today." She glanced at the clock. "After that I think I'll get the camera out and take a few shots. I'm putting together some ideas for a brochure on Hawk's Flight."

Devon didn't get outside with her camera until nearly eleven o'clock. She stepped off the back porch and scanned the peaceful scene in front of her as the dogs greeted her with wagging tails and lolling tongues. Even they seemed relieved there hadn't been another explosion this morning, she thought in amusement. Devon reached down to scratch a few ears. The new barn was more than half completed, she noticed.

She was trying to decide whether to take a few shots of the mares with their foals or to concentrate on one of the stallions when she caught sight of Garth striding out of the old barn. She waved and started toward him.

He halted, leaning against a paddock rail, one booted foot braced on the bottom rung, and watched her approach with gleaming interest in his eyes.

Devon smiled as she took in the sight of him. Garth was wearing jeans that emphasized his lean, strong body. The leather belt around his waist was as scarred and worn as his boots. His shirt was already slightly damp with sweat. It would get far more damp before the day was over. Garth worked harder than any of his men. He had his hat pulled down low over his eyes, shielding himself from the warm, bright morning sunlight. Very much the cowboy, she told herself, and her smile widened. Memories of the previous night flickered through her head. This man was her lover and soon he would be her husband. It made her pulse quicken just to look at him. He never took his eyes off her as she walked up to stand in front of him.

"What are you staring at, cowboy?" she demanded huskily.

Garth used his fist to shove his hat back on his head. He regarded her with a lazy, possessive arrogance that came, Devon knew, from the bone.

"What am I staring at?" he repeated. "Nothing special. Just checkin' over my property."

"Beast!" Devon poked him in the ribs and then hurriedly stepped back out of reach.

"Ouch!" Garth clutched his ribs as though he'd been shot. "What was that all about? You asked a simple question and I gave you a simple answer."

"Hah. You deserved that and you know it. I saw the way you were looking at me."

"Yeah?" He appeared interested. "How was I looking at you?"

"You know exactly how you were looking."

Steve came out of the barn with Ryan at that moment. They took one glance at Garth and Devon and tried to hide their grins. Garth looked at them with a faint frown as they walked toward the new barn. Then he turned back to Devon.

"You ever had the feeling there's a joke going around and everyone else knows the punch line except you?" Garth asked bluntly.

"Uh, yes, occasionally." Ruefully Devon realized the men hadn't been doing a good job of keeping their relief and amusement to themselves.

"That's the way I've been feeling all morning. If some of these fools don't stop grinning behind my back I'm going to drop them into the irrigation canal. What's so damn funny?"

Devon caught more speculative, amused glances from a knot of men who were working on the new barn. She drew a deep breath, wondering how to be diplomatic about this. "I don't think anyone's exactly laughing at you, Garth. They wouldn't dare. They're just relieved."

"Relieved about what, for pete's sake?"

"That you're in a good mood this morning. I think that after last night, they expected you to be chewing nails today."

"So?" he prodded, this time with a hint of aggression. "They ought to be thanking their lucky stars I've decided to let the whole matter drop. I don't see anything humorous about the situation."

Devon cleared her throat. "Yes, well, it's a little hard to explain, Garth. But I think they've all decided they know *why* you're so good-natured today."

"Why?" he repeated ominously.

"Now, Garth, be reasonable. They're men. You know how men are. You're one, yourself, remember? I think they all assume that you and I . . . that is, that we might have, uh . . . well that we did what we did, and that's why you're feeling so much calmer and more cheerful today."

There was a second or two of stunned shock from Garth as the light dawned, and then every vestige of his earlier teasing, easygoing mood vanished as if it had never existed. "I'll flatten each and every one of them."

"Garth! Wait!" Anxiously Devon grabbed his arm as he started to turn toward the nearest victims. The men were standing out of earshot and didn't yet know the lion was again on the prowl.

Garth gave Devon a savage glance. "I won't have them talking about you."

"Garth," Devon said soothingly, "we're going to be married. There's no harm done. Unless, of course, you're thinking of abandoning me at the last moment? That might be a little hard to live down, but otherwise, I don't think there's really a problem. Why are you so concerned if someone thinks we might have slept together?"

"Damn it, Devon, I'm concerned for your sake," he said through his teeth. "I remember how careful you were all those years you were raising Lee and Kurt. You had practically no social life at all because you were so afraid someone would gossip. I'm not going to let them start talking about you now."

She saw the overwhelming protectiveness in his eyes and wanted to throw herself into his arms. "You mean you're not embarrassed about someone thinking we might have gone to bed together?"

"Hell, no! Why should I be embarrassed? Personally, I don't care if the whole damn valley knows. If it was up to me I'd put an announcement on the local radio station. But I know how you always felt about gossip and I won't let you be embarrassed. I'll slaughter any man who opens his mouth about you today, I swear it."

Devon shook her head, her eyes bright with moisture. She stepped close to Garth and wrapped her arms fiercely around his waist. "I don't care if everyone knows, Garth."

"But, Devon, you were always so cautious." Automatically he put his arms around her.

"Only because I didn't want Kurt and Lee to be hurt in any way. I didn't want to put them in a position where they felt they had to defend me and I didn't want them humiliated. I had a responsibility to them."

There was silence from Garth for a long moment. He just stood there holding her to him and then he finally said quietly, "I see."

Devon relaxed. She smiled teasingly into his shirt. "I'm glad you're not too embarrassed about everyone thinking we were together last night. After we're married and sharing the same bedroom it might be a lot tougher to keep everyone from guessing that we occasionally make love. It'll be a great relief not to have to pretend we're above that sort of thing."

Garth gave her a slight shake and then he was laughing into her hair. The deep, vibrant sound made Devon realize how seldom she heard him laugh. She would have to see to it that the event happened more often.

"This is the thanks I get for trying to protect your reputation?" Garth demanded.

"I'm not worried about my reputation as long as the worst thing anyone thinks is that I'm sleeping with you," Devon assured him with a laughing grin. "To be perfectly honest, I'm rather proud of the fact."

"Shameless hussy." He tilted her chin and kissed her soundly, ignoring the fact that Ryan and a handful of construction workers were witnessing the whole thing. When he finally lifted his head, Garth's eyes were brilliant. "You'd better get back to the house before we really give these jokers something to talk about." He gave her a pat on the behind and sent her on her way.

Devon obediently moved off, listening as Garth barked a few orders to the men who had been watching the small scene. His voice was crisp with authority, but there was no anger in it. In fact, Devon decided, Garth sounded quite pleased with himself. She thought about the fact that he'd been trying so hard to protect her reputation, and her love for him warmed her from the crown of her head to the tips of her toes. Garth was a man who would always take care of his wife and family. He would do whatever he had to do in order to protect them.

But, then, she'd known that all along, Devon reminded herself as she opened the screen door and stepped into the kitchen. Garth understood commitment as well as she did.

The sound of Rita Dennison's car in the drive that afternoon came as a pleasant surprise to Devon, who was still mulling over the wedding reception menu. She jumped to her feet and went out onto the front porch to welcome her visitor.

"Rita, come on inside and have some iced tea. Bev and I are still arguing about whether we have to serve roast beef at the reception. I claim the locals can get by for one meal without beef, but Bev doesn't agree."

Rita laughed. "I'm afraid Bev's right. Better have at least a token chunk of beef on the buffet table or everyone will starve." She preceded Devon into the house. "I came by to see what the fallout was from last night.

Everything okay? I felt absolutely terrible about the whole thing."

"You shouldn't be feeling terrible; it was Ordway who started the trouble and Garth who finished it. As far as I can tell, you, as hostess, should be in the clear. Sit down."

"Hostesses are never in the clear." Rita nodded at Bev as she took a seat at the kitchen table. "If nothing else, though, I can rest assured that no one will claim they didn't have a good time last night. Nothing like a little fistfight to entertain the guests."

Bev chuckled as she poured iced tea. "You can say that again. Quite an entertaining evening all around from what I hear."

Rita grimaced. "I'll have to admit that Garth didn't look too thrilled with the whole event. He was absolutely furious, wasn't he? Has he calmed down this morning?"

"He's a different man this morning," Bev assured her with a grin. "Devon soothed all the ruffled feathers last night."

Rita laughed with womanly understanding. "Practicing to be a wife already, Devon? Believe me, after you're married, you'll find yourself spending a heck of a lot of time soothing the savage beast in the old, traditional way. Men are very primitive in a lot of respects. Honestly, they can be so difficult. I don't know why any woman in her right mind gets married. We'd all be a heck of a lot smarter to have a few wild, glorious affairs and forget about trying to actually domesticate the monsters."

Devon grinned. "Your words of wisdom come too late to do me any good."

"Isn't that the truth," Bev acknowledged. "Garth wouldn't let Devon out of this marriage now if she offered to buy her way out with a stallion as well pedigreed as High Flyer or Royal Standard."

"That's what I've heard," Rita said. She looked at Devon with mock sympathy. "I'm afraid you're trapped, Devon. Everyone says Garth waited a whole year for you and he's not about to let you go now."

Out on the back porch Garth stopped short, listening to the laughter of the three women. A sudden, chilled feeling took hold of his insides. Rita's words hammered in his head. *I'm afraid you're trapped, Devon.*

For the first time Garth silently asked the one question he had never allowed himself to ask before. *Why are you marrying me, Devon?* Memories of the previous evening flared in his head. The rush of fury and adrenaline when he'd found Devon struggling in Ordway's arms, the need to smash Ordway's face, the equally fierce need to claim Devon later.

He'd tried to drown that last need with whiskey but it hadn't worked. The moment Devon had opened the study door last night, Garth had known he had to have her. It had been blazingly clear to him that the only way to slake the volatile combination of anger and possessiveness and need that had burned in his veins was to lose himself in Devon's arms.

He'd been right. Afterward the world had settled back down into its proper orbit. The battle was over and he'd reclaimed his woman. She was safe again and so was he.

This morning he'd been feeling so damned good he hadn't even bothered to deliver the lecture he'd planned to give Ryan. Hell, it hardly seemed worth the effort. There was no doubt but that his half brother was feeling guilty enough as it was. Ryan had learned his lesson. There would be no more talk of going into partnership with Phil Ordway.

Garth's hands closed into fists. Consciously he forced himself to relax. He knew why he was marrying Devon. He had to. His world would be a dull, colorless place without her. Physically he was more attracted to her than he'd ever been to any other woman. Emotionally he felt complete around her. And he trusted her.

But why was she marrying him?

Garth stepped silently off the porch, heading back toward High Flyer's paddock. He'd been so certain of the rightness of this marriage, so sure that Devon belonged here with him. He'd overridden all her doubts and extracted a promise from her because he'd been secure in his own belief that she would be happy married to him.

I'm afraid you're trapped, Devon.

She had looked so at home in the city. The day he'd found her in that damn singles bar, Garth had been startled to see how well she blended in with her new surroundings. She hadn't been pining away in San Francisco, that was for certain. She'd found a niche for herself, and if she hadn't been caught by her promise to him, she would undoubtedly have found a man for herself, also.

That last thought made Garth set his teeth. He stopped in front of High Flyer's paddock and stood staring at the dappled gray stallion. The animal was calmly munching hay, arrogant and secure in his natural power and status.

Garth knew he wasn't nearly as handsome as High Flyer, but he was beginning to wonder if he didn't have some of the stallion's arrogance. The thought made him grimace.

Devon could have been happy in the city. She could have found herself a man with a Porsche and a yacht and a country-club membership. She could have made a career out of photography.

But she'd allowed Garth to drag her back to Hawk Springs.

Why?

Because of the promise he'd more or less forced out of her a year ago? But, Garth reminded himself firmly, he'd only gotten that promise out of her because she'd been so lost in her own passion and desire at the time. She responded to him so vibrantly he couldn't believe she didn't want him as much as he wanted her. Hell, he'd even gotten her to admit her desire. She made no secret of it. Last night she'd been on fire with it and she hadn't tried to hide it.

But a woman like Devon wouldn't marry a man just because she liked going to bed with him. She wouldn't let herself be trapped by passion alone.

She might, however, let herself be trapped by a promise she'd been foolish enough to make in the heat of that passion. Devon was the kind of woman who ultimately honored her promises.

He needed her too much to release her from that promise.

"I'm afraid you're trapped, Devon," Garth said aloud.

High Flyer's fine ears flicked briefly in the direction of the man's voice but the stallion didn't interrupt his feeding to investigate further. He had his priorities in life and he didn't pay much attention to distractions.

Garth turned away from the paddock and went to see how the new barn was coming along. A man had priorities in life, too, and he couldn't let himself get distracted or else he'd come apart.

Devon didn't get a chance to talk to Ryan privately until late Tuesday afternoon. He'd been quieter than usual since the events at the Dennisons'. He wasn't sulking or moping, he was just a little withdrawn as though he were doing some major internal reevaluation. She found him shifting bales of hay in one of the barns.

"There you are, Ryan. I've been wanting to talk to you." She ambled over to where he was working and plunked herself down on a hay bale. Ryan took off his hat, wiped his forehead and sat down beside her.

"What's up?" he asked with a curious smile.

"That's what I wanted to ask you. What are your plans now that Ordway's out of the picture?" Devon demanded bluntly.

Ryan lifted one shoulder and let it sink. "I don't know yet. Garth wants me to keep an eye on Hawk's Flight while you two are in Hawaii. When you get back I guess I'll head for L.A. and start job hunting again. Shouldn't be too hard to find something." His mouth curved ruefully. "Present circumstances notwithstanding, I really am pretty good with computers."

"I believe you," Devon said instantly. She smiled. "That's why I wondered if you'd considered another alternative to your original plans to go into partnership with Ordway?"

Ryan slanted her an assessing look. "What alternative?"

"Going into business for yourself. It would have to be on a much smaller scale to begin with, naturally, but it would have potential."

Ryan was silent for a long moment. "Just exactly what did you have in mind?" he finally asked with the first real enthusiasm he'd shown since the night of the Dennisons' party.

Devon told him what she had in mind.

When she was finished Ryan sat looking at her as if she'd taken leave of her senses. "Are you kidding? Garth would go through the roof!"

"Let me talk to him first." Devon jumped down off the stack of hay and waved breezily.

That night she cornered Garth in his study. He looked up with a smile when she sailed through the door but when she sat down on the other side of the desk and told him she wanted to talk about Ryan the smile disappeared.

"Oh, hell." Garth groaned. "I should have known."

"Just hear him out when he explains what he wants to do, Garth. That's all I'm asking. He knows ranching and he knows computers. He can handle this and it'll give him a start in the right direction."

"The last time you asked me a favor like this I wound up having to pull some drunk city dude off of you, remember?"

She ignored the warning in his voice because she could hear the resignation beneath it. Garth was going to give Ryan another chance. Devon grinned. "You won't regret this, Garth, I know it. This time it's going to work out beautifully."

"I wonder if the prospect of getting married makes all men soft in the head, or if it's just me."

"It's probably all men," she assured him. She got up and came around to his side of the desk to drop a quick kiss on his mouth. "Good night, Garth. See you in the morning."

"It's the frustration that does it," he called after her as she headed toward the study door. "I'm going crazy every night alone in my room thinking about you in your bed just down the hall. That's what's making me such a pushover for you and your schemes. I can't think straight because I'm so damned frustrated."

"Is it my fault you're too old-fashioned to have a real, full-blown affair with me before the wedding?" she teased. Then she slipped out into the hall and closed the study door behind her. Devon smiled to herself.

Garth might have stopped worrying excessively about a little gossip but that didn't mean he'd completely changed. He still had old-fashioned ideas about protecting her and equally quaint notions of chivalry and appropriate behavior in one's own home. That meant he wasn't about to make a regular habit of making love to her until they were properly married.

No wonder she loved him, Devon thought. There were probably fewer than a dozen men like him on earth. The species should probably be bred in captivity to assure its survival.

That last thought made Devon catch her breath in sudden realization. Then she smiled smugly. The best thing she could do for womankind was to have Garth's sons. The world needed more men like Garth. Men who could be depended upon when the going got rough. Men who held fast to their own codes of honor. Men who knew how to make a commitment and keep it until the end of time.

For some reason the idea of having Garth's baby no longer seemed like a trap.

Ten

Devon had expected to be able to relax after the wedding. She had counted on the long flight to Hawaii to give her time to unwind from the tension of the ceremony and the boisterous reception that had followed. And she might have been able to calm down if she hadn't become slowly aware of the fact that Garth was acting strangely.

He'd been a solid anchor in the ministorm that had constituted the whole production. Considering the fact that he'd been the least enthusiastic about the size and scale of the thing, he seemed to be the one least traumatized by it all.

When Devon had at last taken her trip down the aisle in front of the assembled crowd, she'd seen the way Garth watched her. There was a lifetime of commitment and desire in his expression. There was also an unyielding possessiveness that had been all the more intense because it was unspoken. She hadn't been able to take her eyes off him as she floated to his side.

When he'd kissed her after the ceremony there had been small murmurs of appreciation and satisfaction from the standing-room-only crowd. Hawk Springs was pleased with the whole event. A sense of approval hung over the gathering and the good wishes had been sincere. Martha Springer hadn't put in an appearance and no one seemed to notice her absence. Devon would never be sure if the woman had stayed away because of the scene at the Dennisons' party or because Garth privately told her not to come. Devon suspected the latter.

Garth had remained calm and unflappable throughout the reception, accepting the comments, jokes and wishes with an easy, polite manner. Devon had been surrounded by a bevy of laughing, teasing women who wanted to know how she'd found herself back in the country after making a successful escape to the city.

"I'll tell you how she got back here," one neighbor announced. "Garth went and got her."

Devon had smiled serenely, her gaze going to her husband who was standing in a crowd of men nearby. Lee and Kurt were in the group, talking easily to people they'd known most of their lives. Ryan was there, too. From what she could overhear they had stopped joking and were busily discussing the weather. Farmers and ranchers never lost an opportunity to worry about the weather. Garth had looked over and caught her eye. He'd nodded once and Devon had known it was his signal to leave. Without any hesitation, she had made her way upstairs to change her clothes.

Bev Middleton had fussed around her as she dressed, telling Devon not to worry about a thing while she was in Hawaii.

"I won't," Devon had assured her lightly as she slipped into the yellow-and-white cotton-knit skirt and top she'd decided to wear on the plane.

"I just hope Garth doesn't fret too much about this place while he's supposed to be enjoying his honeymoon," Bev had continued as she handed Devon a brush.

"He seems to be resigned to leaving Hawk's Flight in Ryan's care for a week," Devon pointed out.

Bev had grinned. "Ryan's like a kid with a new bike. Says he can't wait to start setting up the little computer in Garth's study. I can't believe Garth actually agreed to let him put all the stud farm records on a machine."

Devon laughed. "It will be a perfect opportunity for Ryan to show what he can do. He knows ranching and he knows computers. If anyone can prove that the ranch business can be handled on a computer, it's Ryan. And if he's successful here, other farmers and ranchers in the area will be interested. It could be the start of a very nice business for Ryan."

"And if it is, he'll have you to thank for it," Bev declared shrewdly.

"It's Garth who..."

"Hah," Bev interrupted with a chuckle. "Don't think everyone on the place isn't well aware of the fact that you talked him into giving Ryan the chance. You've got a knack for handling that man. But I guess that's only fair since he seems to have the knack of handling you. Can't think of any other man who could have lured you back to Hawk Springs."

"No," Devon had agreed softly, "there isn't any other man who could have done it."

Lee and Kurt had both kissed her soundly as she stood at the door with Garth. Kurt had smiled his serious smile and told her he was glad she'd finally decided to marry Garth.

"Now we won't have to worry about you getting into trouble in the big city," her brother had teased.

"I never had any trouble at all in the big city," Devon had retorted, conscious of Garth waiting impatiently for her to say her goodbyes.

"Maybe that's what had us all worried," Lee had remarked. He'd exchanged a man-to-man look with Garth over the top of Devon's head. "You seemed to be getting on a little too well. Right, Garth?"

"She's home now," was all Garth had said in reply but there'd definitely been a hint of steel underlying the words.

Garth had said little on the way to the airport but Devon had been too wound up from the morning's hectic events to notice. She'd chatted easily about everything from the success of the food to her plans for the new advertising brochure she was putting together for Hawk's Flight. Garth had seemed content to let her talk but he'd added little to the conversation.

Halfway out over the Pacific Devon had finally settled down enough to notice that something was definitely wrong. When the realization had sunk in she hadn't known what to say. The middle of a crowded 747 was hardly the place to begin an in-depth discussion of what had gone awry with a marriage that was only a few hours old. Gradually she had become as silent as Garth. By the time they reached the luxurious Waikiki beachfront hotel, neither of them was saying much of anything.

She watched as Garth tipped the bellboy and then closed the door firmly behind him. He walked back across the room and opened the sliding glass door that opened onto a private balcony. As he stepped outside into the velvet Hawaiian evening, he undid the knot in the tie he'd been wearing most of the day. With the silk ends hanging loose, he planted both hands on the railing and stood contemplating the moonlit sea.

Devon hesitated a moment, aware of a new kind of nervousness pervading her body. She'd been tense and excited during the wedding and reception, and she'd been uneasy about Garth's quiet mood on the plane. But this new sensation was something altogether different. Devon licked her dry lips and realized she was suddenly a little frightened.

Something was wrong and Garth wasn't telling her what that something was.

Quietly Devon moved out onto the balcony beside her husband, not touching him. She followed his gaze out to sea. "It's very beautiful, isn't it?"

"It isn't Hawk Springs," he agreed laconically.

Devon's fingers tightened on the railing. "No, it isn't Hawk Springs." She sighed. "Is that what's bothering you, Garth? Have you started worrying already about the stud farm?"

"Devon..."

"I should have known this wouldn't work," she continued sadly. "I should have realized you couldn't be forced to take a vacation."

"Devon..."

"I thought that once I got you away from Hawk's Flight, you'd be able to relax and enjoy the first real vacation you've had in years. I thought we could use the time to get to know each other without having someone else always around. But it was a mistake, wasn't it? We should've spent the weekend in Santa Barbara looking at land and horses."

"Devon, why did you—" Garth tried again, only to be interrupted as Devon went on with her self-directed chastisement.

"We don't have to stay here a whole week, Garth. We can fly back to California tomorrow. I shouldn't have pushed you into this. It was a mistake, but we don't have to go on with it."

Garth came away from the railing with a swift, impatient movement, catching her by the shoulders and pulling her around to face him. "Will you please stop babbling about what a mistake this all was and tell me why you married me?"

She stared up at him, dumbfounded. "Why I married you?"

"Yes, damn it, give it to me straight," he said fiercely. "I have to know. I told myself it didn't matter. I was sure we could make a go of things once I had you back at Hawk's Flight. I was so sure of what I was doing that I didn't allow myself to consider the fact that I might be wrong."

"Wrong? But, Garth . . ."

"I still think that marrying me was the right thing for you to do, but for the past few days it's been eating at me."

"What's been eating at you?" she demanded.

"I can handle most things, Devon, as long as I can face them head on. But I have to know what I'm supposed to deal with before I can figure out how to manage it. So tell me why you married me. Was it because you felt you couldn't go back on the promise you gave me a year ago? Or was it because you felt you owed me something for helping you out when Lee got into trouble? Just tell me the truth, Devon. I can take it from there. But I have to know why you let me put that ring on your finger today."

She was shaken by the intensity of the demand. "Does it matter, Garth?" she whispered.

"It matters," he said through his teeth. "Believe me, it matters."

Devon drew in her breath and touched his hard jaw with the tips of her fingers. It was safe to trust Garth with the truth. He wouldn't use it against her or taunt her with it. He was an honest man who respected honesty in others. And he would respect her feelings for him, even if he couldn't return them in full measure.

"I'm not quite noble or self-sacrificing enough to marry a man because I made a rash promise during a moment of passion. Nor am I the kind of woman who would repay a debt by marrying a man who'd done her a favor, even though the favor was a very big one. I married you because I love you, Garth. No other reason."

His hands tightened convulsively on her shoulders. "You love me?"

"Oh, yes. I love you." She smiled mistily. "I didn't want to admit it a year ago because I had to get away from Hawk Springs for a while. I had to have some time to myself. I had been feeling so trapped for so long that I was on the verge of panic. My life was flipping by and I hadn't had a chance to really live. I told myself I couldn't trust my responses to you because I had too many other things going on in my head. I was confused and desperate and tired from the strain of looking after Lee and Kurt. I was sure that what I felt for you couldn't be love. You were the wrong man and Hawk Springs was definitely the wrong place for me. I'd been telling myself all those things for so long I believed them. I decided that what I felt for you was only passion combined with friendship."

"Maybe that's all it was, Devon."

She shook her head, not quite managing to suppress a very womanly smile. "Even if it had been, that would have been better grounds for a marriage than most people have. But I've got news for you, Garth Saxon. No woman waits a whole year for a man just because he was good in bed. Not when she's got other choices and other opportunities."

"Don't remind me," he muttered.

She ignored that. "When I saw you at Christmas time and realized I really was waiting, I knew I had a problem. I hadn't wanted any other man to even try to get close to me. I kept telling myself it was because deep down I didn't want to marry anyone. My freedom was too precious to me and even if I did eventually decide to marry, I was sure I didn't want to marry a rancher."

"From Hawk Springs." Garth's mouth twisted wryly.

Devon laughed up at him with her eyes. "Most especially not one from Hawk Springs."

"But you let me bring you back at the end of the year."

"I went with you because when I saw you in that singles bar three weeks ago I knew deep down I had no choice. I realized a part of me had always been waiting for you to come and bring me home. I dragged my feet a little and I argued and tried to think of reasons why we shouldn't get married because the logical part of me still wasn't sure of what I wanted, but in the end I went with you. I loved you and I was finally admitting it to myself. Once I'd faced that fact, I knew where I belonged."

"With me." Garth's eyes were gleaming in the shadows. He lifted his hands to gently frame her face. Devon realized his strong fingers were trembling slightly and she wondered if some of the brilliance in his eyes was the dampness of unshed tears. The love she was feeling seemed to overflow her body, reaching out to engulf him.

"Oh, Garth," she breathed, wrapping him tightly around the waist. "I love you so much."

"Not half as much as I love you." His voice was dark and thick with emotion as he folded her close against his warmth.

Devon stood very still, hardly daring to breath. "You do?"

He nodded into her hair. "I didn't worry about that end of things. I didn't think it was important. There were other factors that were a lot more crucial. I wanted you and that night before you left Hawk Springs I'd proved to myself that I could make you want me. You'll never know how hard I hung on to that knowledge during this past year. I prayed you'd remember it, too."

"I was stuck with the memory, believe me," she confessed on a soft, muffled laugh.

His fingers worked gently on her spine. "I'm glad. In addition to telling myself I could make you want me, I knew I could trust you, and God knows after what I'd been through in my first marriage, trust was important to me. I knew you'd do everything you could to make the marriage work once you'd committed yourself to it and to me. I knew the kind of commitment you were capable of making because I'd seen what you'd done for your brothers. I was sure you'd do even more for a husband and a family of your own. I thought all I had to do was tie a few knots around you to make you realize you belonged with me. I was certain you'd adapt easily to the ranch. You'd grown up on a farm and you knew what life in the country was all about. It wouldn't come as any great shock to you if someone accidentally tramped horse manure onto the back porch."

"In other words," Devon dared to say teasingly, "you thought you had everything worked out logically and for the good of all concerned."

He groaned and hugged her so tightly she squeaked. "I'm afraid so. But that day after the Dennisons' party I heard Rita talking in the kitchen, telling you that you were trapped. It suddenly hit me that I didn't want you to feel trapped. I wanted you to stay with me because you wanted to be with me. I wanted you to love me. And when I realized that, I knew I loved you, too. Then I started to really worry."

"I didn't hear any last-minute offers of a reprieve," Devon couldn't resist saying. "You didn't suggest we talk things over or wait until we were sure of what we were doing."

"I said I started to worry," he told her bluntly, "I didn't say I changed my mind."

She smiled into his shirt. "No, of course not."

"Devon, I would have gone through with this marriage even if I'd had to hog-tie you and drag you down the aisle. I couldn't have taken the risk of letting you go away again. But today I realized I needed to know the exact truth. I wanted to know where we stood with each other so I could start working on making you fall in love with me. But I haven't known how to ask. I've spent most of the day trying to figure out a way to bring up the subject. Then you went and started blathering on about this honeymoon being a mistake, and all of a sudden it was all out in the open."

"I'm glad," she murmured. "Just think, we might have spent our whole honeymoon wondering if we were in love."

He pushed her a little away from him so he could smile down into her face. "Somehow, I think we would have figured it out before the week was over."

"Maybe, but personally I'm glad we've got it figured out tonight." She put her arms around his neck. "Although, to tell you the truth, we both should have figured it out long ago. Any man and woman who wait a year for each other must be feeling something fairly strong."

"Either that or they're just not too bright," Garth offered with a slow grin.

She answered his smile and then shook her head. "I told myself you were a man and you wouldn't wait a year for any woman. When I knew you'd waited for me, I should have realized you loved me."

"Don't ever doubt it again." He kissed her with a rough, hungry passion that told its own story. "I don't know how I survived that year. I don't know how I survived the past three weeks, for that matter. I give you fair warning, sweetheart. I'm never going to let you go again. You belong to me."

"I couldn't leave you again, Garth. Home for me is wherever you are. It always will be."

He muttered her name against her mouth and then he was lifting her high in his arms. He carried her back into the room, laying her down on the bed with great care. Devon reached for him, welcoming her husband into her heart, and Garth came to her with all the strength, tenderness and passion that characterized his nature.

There were few words between them this time as the loving excitement flowed around them. It was a time of mutual claiming and silent promise. Devon was enthralled with the overwhelming sense of possessing and being possessed, of loving and being loved completely in return. Hearts, minds and bodies pulsed, shuddered and finally flamed in a release that left Devon locked securely in Garth's arms. When it was over she curled trustingly into his embrace, held close to his side.

For a long while they lay quietly together in the warm Hawaiian night, letting the peaceful aftermath cradle them. Garth's rough fingertips moved in an absent caress on Devon's arm. His eyes were gleaming with love and gentleness as he looked down at her.

"I haven't had the nerve to ask if you're pregnant," he admitted softly.

Devon stretched luxuriously beside him. "No." She smiled. "But it would be okay if I was. Better than okay. I've decided I would very much like to have your baby."

"Devon." He exhaled deeply, holding her with fierce pleasure and thankfulness. "I love you so much."

The silent communion of trust and love was broken sometime later when Garth stirred lazily and asked, "Hungry?"

Devon's fingers tangled lightly in the hair on his chest. "No. Are you?"

He shook his head, watching her with deep pleasure. "No. Not yet. We can get a bite later or have something sent up from room service."

"Room service!" Her shock was only part pretense. "You'd actually indulge yourself with room service? What a waste of money, Garth. Shocking."

"I figure we've already blown so much cash on this trip to Hawaii, a few more bucks for room service won't matter. Besides—" he turned onto his side and gave her a meaningful smile "—I don't feel like leaving this room tonight. I'm willing to pay for the privilege of having you all to myself."

Devon shivered with delight at the look in his eyes. She moved languidly, invitingly against him. "I don't feel like going out for dinner either."

"Good." He nodded and bent his head to brush his mouth against her lips. "We'll spend tonight here, then. Tomorrow we can hop a flight over to the big island. I understand there's an interesting cattle ranch there and there's also some land for sale. I saw the ads in the back of the in-flight magazine."

"A cattle ranch! *Land for sale?*" Devon shot bolt upright in bed. "What do you think you're up to, cowboy? This is our honeymoon. We're not here to shop for land or tour cattle ranches. I didn't drag you all this way just so you could look at property and cows on our honeymoon. You can do that anytime. I'm the one who arranged this trip. I'm the one who organized the whole thing. We're going to spend the week honeymooning my way and that's final! We're going to eat pineapple and poi and watch hula dances and swim in the sea. Look at property, my foot. Of all the nerve . . ." She broke off abruptly as she realized he was laughing down at her.

"I've decided I have to make a few demands. I don't want you getting the idea you can wrap me completely around your little finger," Garth teased.

"What?" She feigned total astonishment.

"You know damn well that's what everyone back in Hawk Springs has decided. Bev, Ryan, Steve, Cal and everyone else think you're definitely the power behind the throne at Hawk's Flight. They think you've got me dancing on your string. That you can get just about anything you want out of me. That I'll do anything for you."

Devon smiled enticingly up at him. She sank her fingertips into his hair. "Well?"

"Well what?" He kissed the tip of her breast and watched in satisfaction as the nipple began to harden.

"Are they right?"

"Umm. Probably." He kissed the other breast.

"You don't look all that worried about it," Devon noted.

Garth grinned, a wicked, sexy grin that was part male arrogance, part teasing indulgence, part desire and one hundred percent love. "I'm not. Because it works both ways."

"You think you can get just about anything you want from me?" she murmured with deep interest.

"As long as I have you, I have everything I want." Garth ended the conversation very decisively by covering Devon's mouth with his own.

Devon sighed with pleasure, put her arms around her husband and did what she always did around Garth Saxon. She surrendered to the inevitable.

* * * * *

GO WILD WITH

Desire

Just as the hero and heroine at the end of a Silhouette Desire have made a commitment to each other, Silhouette Desire is committed to bringing you the six best romances we can find every month.

SAXON'S LADY by **Stephanie James** is your special introduction to a world of passion and enchantment. The six provocative, emotion-packed Silhouette Desires available each month will take you across America, around the world and·into the hearts and souls of fascinating characters.

The Silhouette Desire line presents a variety of authors, writing styles and types of stories, written for every woman that you are, yet it never fails to deliver a sensuous, contemporary romance. The line is a blend of both new and familiar authors, and combines stories that are light and humorous with ones that are emotional and poignant, compelling and believable, or playful and fanciful.

SDS1-2

Diana Palmer, Annette Broadrick, Joan Hohl,
Ann Major, Elizabeth Lowell and Erin St. Claire
are masters of the high-powered, emotional
romance. Dixie Browning, Jennifer Greene, Lass
Small, Jo Ann Algermissen, Robin Elliott and
Joyce Thies use humor and a lighter touch to
entertain and captivate you.

These authors write stories that will make you
laugh, make you cry—stories that will touch your
heart—about the allure of living a dream or the
troubles and triumphs of reaching out and
achieving one.

Silhouette Desires are written with you, today's
woman, in mind. They are believable, sensuous
love stories. If you want to experience firsthand
all the excitement, passion and pure joy of falling
in love, join us . . . go wild with Silhouette Desire!

Silhouette Desire

Silhouette Desire

Indulge yourself.
Discover the unique blend
of fantasy and reality
in these sensuous romances.
Recapture the love.

READERS' COMMENTS ON SILHOUETTE DESIRES

"Thank you for Silhouette Desires. They are the best thing that has happened to the bookshelves in a long time."
— V.W.*, Knoxville, TN

"Silhouette Desires—wonderful, fantastic—the best romance around."
— H.T.*, Margate, N.J.

"As a writer as well as a reader of romantic fiction, I found DESIREs most refreshingly realistic—and definitely as magical as the love captured on their pages."
— C.M.*, Silver Lake, N.Y.

"I just wanted to let you know how very much I enjoy your Silhouette Desire books. I read other romances, and I must say your books rate up at the top of the list."
— C.N.*, Anaheim, CA

"Desires are number one. I especially enjoy the endings because they just don't leave you with a kiss or embrace; they finish the story. Thank you for giving me such reading pleasure."
— M.S.*, Sandford, FL

*names available on request

FOUR UNIQUE SERIES
FOR EVERY WOMAN YOU ARE..

Silhouette Romance

Heartwarming romances that will make you laugh and cry as they bring you all the wonder and magic of falling in love.

6 titles per month

Silhouette Special Edition

Expanded romances written with emotion and heightened romantic tension to ensure powerful stories. A rare blend of passion and dramatic realism.

6 titles per month

Silhouette Desire

Believable, sensuous, compelling—and above all, romantic—these stories deliver the promise of love, the guarantee of satisfaction.

6 titles per month

Silhouette Intimate Moments

Love stories that entice; longer, more sensuous romances filled with adventure, suspense, glamour and melodrama.

4 titles per month

Silhouette Romances
not available in retail outlets in Canada

SIL-GEN-1A